WAITING
FOR
AUTUMN

WAITING FOR AUTUMN

scott blum

HAY HOUSE, INC.
Carlsbad, California • New York City
London • Sydney • Johannesburg
Vancouver • Hong Kong • New Delhi

Published and distributed in the United States by: Hay House, Inc.: www.hayhouse.com • *Published and distributed in Australia by:* Hay House Australia Pty. Ltd.: www.hayhouse.com.au • *Published and distributed in the United Kingdom by:* Hay House UK, Ltd.: www.hay house.co.uk • *Published and distributed in the Republic of South Africa by:* Hay House SA (Pty), Ltd.: www.hayhouse.co.za • *Distributed in Canada by:* Raincoast: www.raincoast.com • *Published in India by:* Hay House Publishers India: www.hayhouse.co.in

Design: Amy Rose Grigoriou

Library of Congress Cataloging-in-Publication Data

Blum, Scott.
  Waiting for autumn / Scott Blum.
     p. cm.
  ISBN 978-1-4019-2270-2 (hardcover : alk. paper) 1. Young adults--Fiction. 2. Ashland (Or.)--Fiction. 3. Spiritual direction--Fiction. 4. New Age fiction. I. Title.
  PS3602.l864W35 2009
  813'.6--dc22

                                            2008022273

ISBN: 978-1-4019-2270-2

12 11 10 09   4 3 2 1
1st edition, April 2009

Printed in the United States of America

PREFACE

Many people have asked me if the following story is fact or fiction, and I always find that a difficult question to answer. The truth for me is not limited by the physical world, but is instead embodied by energy, floating in the gaps between time and space on that elusive river of intention. And the energy contained in these pages is as real as any light I have seen, song I have heard, or fruit I have tasted. It is true that I have used a fictional thread to stitch these words together into a fabric that is easier to appreciate, and it's also true that many of the events described have actually happened in a form most people could relate to. But for me that is of little importance, as the underlying energy is, and has always been, my truth.

I hope you will enjoy reading my truth and will soon be inspired to listen to your own.

CHAPTER ONE

He was the happiest homeless person I had ever seen. His smile was warm and friendly, and his shoulder-length hair matched his matted red beard. Although he seemed to be wearing the same ratty brown clothes from the day before and smelled like he hadn't bathed in a week, something about his water-blue eyes put me at ease.

As I carried my groceries across the Co-op parking lot, I read the hand-lettered cardboard sign he was holding:

Always receive with grace.

His smile widened knowingly as I walked past, and when I looked down, I noticed a small black puppy asleep at his feet. Once I was nearly past him, I whispered to myself, "That's ironic."

"What's ironic?" he asked.

Startled, I took another step, hoping to act like I didn't hear him.

"What's ironic?" he repeated.

I stopped and slowly turned around. Embarrassed, I said, "It's ironic that you're giving advice on how to receive, when you're asking for money."

"I'm not asking for anything," he smirked. "Right now I'm giving."

I took the bait without even thinking. "So when are you going to give *me* something?"

"I already have, but you wouldn't accept it in the manner it was offered."

"Oh, I think you're mistaken—you definitely haven't given me anything. Perhaps you confused me with someone else."

"No, I didn't confuse you with anyone else!" He was clearly annoyed. "Please leave now; I'm very busy."

I looked around and there wasn't anyone within 100 yards of us.

"Please leave now," he repeated and turned away from me.

Embarrassed, I carried my groceries up the hill to my apartment. I didn't know what I'd said to offend him, but he clearly wasn't happy with the way I had handled myself.

When I returned to the apartment, I was still profoundly disturbed by what had happened. I tried to shake it off and convince myself that he was probably just confusing me with someone else. I wanted to forget about it and go on with my day, but I simply couldn't. I didn't usually care what other people thought of me, but I had a strange connection to him and didn't want to let it go.

Less than an hour later, I picked up my wallet and made my way back down the hill. I wasn't sure what I was going to say, but I had to *try*.

I was relieved to see his matted red hair and his small black puppy as I approached the Co-op. As I got closer, I saw that he had a new sign that read:

I want an orange.
What do you want?

I smiled and thought that this was a good idea for a peace offering. I went into the store and bought the best navel I could find and picked up a few odds and ends I hadn't had room to carry before.

As I passed through the glass double doors, I tossed him the orange and decided to give it another shot. "Here you go," I said as the orange left my hand.

"Thanks." He smiled, and genuinely seemed grateful for the orange. "That's the best thing that happened to me all day."

His words instantly made me feel much better, and I decided to be a bit playful.

"So you can help me get what I want?" I smirked.

"Of course I can."

"How can you do that?"

"You can manifest anything you want."

"Oh, really? Why don't *you* do it?"

"I do, every day."

"Then why are you still homeless?"

"Why do you think I'm homeless?"

Oh dear, I thought. I would definitely need to watch my words more carefully if I was going to spend more time with him.

"What do you manifest?" I asked, trying my best to change the subject.

"Today I manifested an orange."

I laughed. "All you did was write a sign that said you wanted an orange."

"And you gave me one. So clearly I was successful at manifesting." He smiled proudly.

"So if I want a million dollars, all I have to do is make a sign that says 'Give me a million dollars' and someone will just give it to me?"

"Do you believe that will happen?"

"Of course not! There's no way some guy is going to see a sign and give me a million bucks!"

"Then you answered your own question."

"So you agree—you can't just make anything you want appear out of nowhere."

"No. I simply agree *you* don't believe that's the right way to manifest a million dollars. Manifesting isn't about making a halfhearted effort and then failing. Manifesting is about aligning your goals and your destiny so they become one. You have to believe without a doubt and act without pause, or else you're wasting your time. Do you really want a million dollars?"

"Of course I do."

"I don't believe you."

"Why not?"

"Because I have an orange, and it doesn't look like you have anywhere near a million dollars in your pocket."

Perhaps he had a point.

"What do you *really* want?" His eyes felt like they were drilling holes straight through me.

"To be happy," I answered after a long pause.

"Now *that's* something I can help you with. Once you're honest with yourself, you're halfway there.

"I'm Robert," he said with his hand outstretched.

"I'm Scott." I shook his hand.

"Nice to meet you, Scott. And this is my puppy, Don. Come back here tomorrow around the same time, and I'll have something for you."

As I walked away, I was both intrigued by and afraid of how drawn to Robert I was. There was something foreign to me about how open and warm people in Ashland were, and I was still getting used to it. Back in Los Angeles, I had grown comfortable with the blanket of anonymity provided by the city crowds. And when I first discovered how friendly the people were in this small mountain town of southern Oregon, I felt ashamed by how closed off I had become over the years and vowed to open back up. In this town, nobody knew how jaded and distrusting I'd been in L.A., and I wanted to reinvent myself as a friendly person who only saw the good in others. It was a great mental exercise and almost immediately began to give me back some of the optimism of my childhood. I decided to hold on to that ideal as I made my way back up the hill and continued to unpack more boxes.

🍁

I loved my new apartment, and it was in a great location, only three short blocks from Lithia Park in the northerly hills above downtown Ashland. Tucked between mature oaks on a tree-lined street, the pale yellow duplex was much larger than I was used to and seemed more like a house than an apartment—especially with its huge backyard. The bedroom had a great view, and the apartment was also month-to-month, so if Ashland didn't work out, I could always continue on my journey north and wouldn't be stuck there for more than a month at a time.

A few days earlier I had been on my way to Portland to start my life over after once again losing my job in the coldhearted entertainment industry. Ever since I moved to Los Angeles, a string of bad luck prevented me from keeping a job for more than a few months at a time. There were always budget reasons, but the truth was, I never found a niche in any of the companies I worked at and was always the first to go if times got tough. And because I had a knack for always picking the wrong employer, I would be out of work more often than not.

Finally, I promised myself that if I lost my job again, I would leave the city before my savings dwindled to the point where I would never be able to do so. Luckily, one of the first people I'd met in Los Angeles was a young, ambitious band manager named Clark. He worked at the same record label I did when I first arrived in L.A., and he was always working on a get-rich-quick scheme. We hit it off pretty quickly, but when we met, he was already on his way out. He'd had his fill of the Hollywood scene and decided to move to Portland to start an independent record label to take advantage of the city's burgeoning music scene. He had offered me a job as soon as he got his new company set up in Oregon, and I finally decided to take him up on it after I received my most recent two weeks' notice. I just threw everything I could fit into a U-Haul trailer and started driving north. I was gone within a day of losing my job, without even bothering to say goodbye to anyone I knew.

After driving twelve hours straight, I crossed the California-Oregon border, and my old Volvo dramatically died on the Siskiyou mountain pass after a loud explosion and a huge plume of thick black smoke. I should have stopped at a gas station to check my car before starting up the summit, as I was already familiar with how hard the Siskiyous were on old cars. I'd grown up in a small town in Northern California about fifty miles south of the Oregon border, so I had scaled that very mountain pass many times. However, my family had moved to the Midwest several years before, and all of my old friends were long gone, so there was no reason to stop on my way through. Although in retrospect, double-checking the oil in Yreka would have been a good idea.

Luckily, a highway patrol was just a few miles behind me when my car exploded, and he blocked off the narrow lane it was in until the tow truck arrived. I had my car and trailer towed to the first available mechanic, who was in Ashland. And when I found out how much it was going to cost to fix the car, I needed to decide if I was going to get a bus ticket to Portland or spend all of my savings to resuscitate my Volvo.

I nearly bought a bus ticket out of Ashland, but something told me I should put off the decision for a few days and just stay put. I hadn't really been attached to Portland as much as I just wanted to get out of L.A. Although I technically already had a job waiting for me up there, I had enough money to support myself for a few months while I tried to find work.

I'd forgotten how much I liked Ashland—it was one of my favorite places from when I was younger. I remembered visiting the idyllic tourist town to go shopping, eat at restaurants, or see an occasional Shakespeare play. The town was beautiful, the air was clean, it had culture, and most important, I simply liked it. I felt *comfortable* in Ashland, and I hadn't felt comfortable in any place (including my own skin) since before I could remember.

After I found myself stranded in Ashland for a few days, life instantly seemed much easier, and I quickly abandoned my original plan and decided to stay in southern Oregon. I was already much happier than I had ever been in L.A., and soon I even got used to the idea of living without a car. I'd been on foot the entire time since I had arrived, and it was liberating to be car free after being bound for so many years.

CHAPTER TWO

The next day I woke up on top of the world. I was still shredded from moving and unpacking, but my adrenal reserves kept me mobile, as I was officially living in the most beautiful town I'd ever been in. Since I'd arrived, the weather had been unusually hot and sometimes even rivaled the peak summer temperatures of Southern California. It was a good thing, too, because my wardrobe had diminished to primarily short-sleeve T-shirts, blue jeans, and tennis shoes over the years of working in the casual environment of the entertainment industry. The locals warned me that the temperature would plummet once the seasons changed, and I began to look forward to it, since I'd been living in a single season for the past several years.

Around the same time as on the previous day, I returned to the Co-op, excited to see what my new friend would have for me. Robert was sitting cross-legged, with his back propped against a conifer and the little black Lab sleeping at his feet. He was still wearing the same ripped brown clothes from the day before, although it looked like he might have found a brush for his hair. As I approached, the puppy opened his eyes to briefly acknowledge my presence, but he quickly squinted them shut and returned to his seemingly perpetual sleep.

"Hi," I said as I walked toward them.

"Hello, Scott." Robert stood up quickly, gathered his belongings, and began to put them in his large canvas bag. He casually tossed the freshly lettered cardboard sign he was holding to the ground.

There is no difference between
_____ and _____.

His sign challenged me. I knew I could find a pair that would clearly disprove his apparent premise of equality and started running through various odd couples in my mind. Giraffes and alligators. Debutantes and automobiles. Windows and feathers.

I finally said one aloud that was sure to stump him: "Elbows and mushrooms."

"Pardon me?"

"Your sign—there is no difference between elbows and mushrooms," I said smugly.

"I agree." He continued packing. "Of course there's not."

His answer confused me, and as I began to protest, he shook his head as if to say, *Don't bother; you have so much to learn.*

He then slid the sign into his backpack and carefully arranged a family of miscellany within the drawstring bag. He held it out to me and asked, "Do you mind?"

"Sure." I grabbed the cloth bag and slung it over my shoulder, although my ego was still a bit dented from his dismissive response.

"Let's go," he said as he swung the puppy over his shoulder like he was burping a furry baby. The small dog let out a soft whimper of surprise as his underside landed on Robert's shoulder, but his eyelids remained shut, and he quickly returned to his state of indifference.

We walked up the hill to Main Street and turned right at the base of the hill next to the large gray library. I had never been inside the public building before, but its imposing presence confidently presided over the south side of downtown.

"Where are we headed?" I asked.

Robert shot me a sharp glance, making it clear that my question wasn't going to be answered. For a brief moment I wondered if I could trust him, since he seemed to have a habit of being secretive and cryptic on occasion. But the truth was that I felt comfortable when I was around him. It was as if all was as it was supposed to be, and he conveyed a certain childlike innocence that made everything seem okay. Although it didn't make a lot of sense to trust someone so completely whom I'd just met, I decided to write off my apprehension as leftover mistrust from L.A. If I was going to stay in Ashland, I would need to make some friends anyway, so I tried to put the doubts out of my mind and enjoy the day without thinking too much about it.

"Where are you from?" I asked, changing the subject.

"I'm from all over, most recently from Eugene."

"And what brought you here?"

"I came to meet you, of course."

I laughed, not sure if he was joking.

"I travel to wherever I'm needed, and Ashland always seems to have people who are ready to move on to the next level."

"The next level of what?"

"The next level of consciousness. Because Ashland is in a vortex, it traps people who are on the path. And many, like you, don't realize they're on a path until they meet someone like me."

"Someone like you? What does that mean? You mean there are other people like you?"

"Of course there are other people like me, just as there are other people like you. You are on the verge of a spiritual awakening, and I'm here to help you through it. Thankfully, many people are on their way, now more than ever. It's finally time for this planet to wake up so we can collectively progress to the next level."

I didn't think I was on the verge of a spiritual anything. I simply thought that my car had broken down in a small mountain town, and I was trying to make the best of it with what little money I had. I'd never really thought much about spirituality before, and although my parents had both been brought up in religious families, they decided to raise their kids to be agnostic, so I didn't have much experience with such things. And although we celebrated Christmas, it was much more "Santa & Rudolph" than "Jesus & Mary."

As we continued to walk up into the hills above the town center, I finally realized why Robert was being so nice. He was evidently a religious fanatic trying to convert me.

"So what religion are you?" I thought that it was time to get it out into the open.

"Religion? I'm not religious!" he answered indignantly. "Who said anything about religion? Spirituality and religion are two very different things."

"Sorry, I just thought—"

"Religion is the *knowledge* of truth," he interrupted, "and spirituality is the *wisdom* of truth."

"Are you saying that religious people aren't spiritual?" I was confused.

"Of course not." His voice became much softer and more understanding as he explained further: "There are lots of religious people who are very spiritual. Religion is just one of the many paths to spiritual awakening. Memorizing passages, practicing rituals, or studying the science of the universe all do the same thing: they keep the mind occupied with knowledge until one has enough life experience to know what to do with it. And that is wisdom. *Wisdom = Knowledge + Experience.*"

"But if religion is the knowledge of truth, how can so many religious books contradict each other?" My agnostic upbringing was starting to show.

"There is a single underlying truth that ties everyone together, whether it's written or not. And although they try, words always fall short of capturing the *essence* of truth, and contradiction is one of their first traps."

I was starting to get dizzy, and I waved for Robert to stop so that I could catch my breath before continuing. I'd thought that I was in pretty good shape, but all those years of sitting in bumper-to-bumper traffic had clearly taken their toll.

Robert put the small black puppy down on the sidewalk and continued: "But for those of us who are open to tapping into the wisdom of the universe that already exists, we can embark on the path of truth in much less time."

I resumed walking slowly up the steep hill, and after making sure the puppy was okay, Robert flung the black Lab over his shoulder and effortlessly jogged up the hill to catch up with me.

After letting what he said sink in, I finally asked, "So does that mean *I* can tap into wisdom of the universe?"

"Yes, you can. We all can. The question is: *are you ready to surrender your own experiences to the universe?*" He held my gaze intensely for several seconds, and I looked away.

"That sounds hard," I finally said.

"What's *hard* is fighting against destiny. But that's what making mistakes is for. To learn what is and what isn't your destiny. Do you understand?"

"Yes. No. I don't know." I didn't have any energy to pretend.

"That's what I like about you," he laughed. "Your honesty is refreshing."

I didn't know what to say that would make it any clearer, so I finally asked, "How long have you been helping people with their spiritual awakening?"

"About 1,200 years now."

I nearly tripped on the curb, not sure if I'd heard him right. "You look pretty good for 1,200 years old."

"Very funny. Of course I haven't been in *this* body for 1,200 years. This one is pretty new to me."

"How new?"

"Just a few weeks now. I got it in Eugene from Don here," he said, gesturing to his small furry companion, whose eyes were now half open as the puppy's head bobbed up and down with Robert's every step.

"Puppy Don gave you the body you're in now? How did that work?"

"'Puppy Don'—I like that." He smiled. "I'm what they call a *Walk-in*," he continued. "What that means is, I look for a host body to use whenever my previous body is no longer of service and then use the new one. It's very similar to what everyone else does before they're born, but instead of my soul picking a newly conceived body, I pick one that already knows how to walk and talk. It makes it a lot easier to get down to business. After 1,200 years, I don't need to be a teenager again. That's too much distraction."

My head was spinning. I wasn't sure if I believed him or not, but I had to admit he wasn't boring.

"And what does Puppy Don have to do with all this?"

"This body I'm in was previously inhabited by Don. Unfortunately, the cancer got to him, and he couldn't afford the treatment. And since he was so entrenched in the illusion of modern medicine, he didn't realize he could treat himself. So when he was on his way out, I made a deal with him that I would give him another body and take care of him if I could use his human one."

"So you turned him into a dog?"

"Of course not!" he laughed. "I just gave his soul some options that were most practical, and after some convincing, he selected the body he's in now. I'm not going to be in this body very long, so he needed to pick one that was on the same cycle that I was."

"He needed to live in dog years."

"Exactly."

After scaling the second hill, I was nearly out of breath again and wasn't sure that I could make it up the third. Robert handed me an unopened bottle of water, and I took a sip, which gave me a chance to take in the beautiful vista of the valley. The water was exceptionally refreshing, and looking down the hill, we paused long enough so that I could see the floor of the valley below that seemed to cuddle up to the hills like a hand-woven rug next to a stately stone hearth. There were many places I had never been to in Ashland, and I was always taken by the town's beauty when I discovered a new vantage point to view it from.

"Here we are," Robert said when we arrived at the top of the third hill. In front of us was a large cement-covered water reservoir, and to the right the road turned from pavement to dirt and meandered through what seemed to be a horse pasture. I followed Robert off the main road to the left and came to the top of a hidden stairway that had been obscured by several full bushes. We carefully descended the precarious steps into the most magical meadow I had ever seen. Shafts of golden light danced on the moss-covered fallen logs, and the ground was carpeted with a combination of long green grass and the most delicate of ivy.

"This is incredible," I gasped while taking in the magical beauty that appeared to have been lifted from a Maxfield Parrish painting. The light that engulfed the meadow was in constant motion, and the hues of the trees and grasses changed from blue to green to purple to orange and back again.

"Yes, it is. This is the largest fairy meadow in all of Ashland. Be sure to stay on the path as you walk—you don't want to crush anyone's home."

I wasn't sure when he was serious or not, but judging by his wrinkled brow, it didn't *seem* like he was joking.

"You wanted to learn how to gather universal wisdom that already exists, and that is why I brought you here. Nature is filled with *that* very wisdom, and it's all around us every day. There are many wise nature spirits living in this meadow, so it's an easy place to feel the difference between their energy and the energy created by humans. Be very quiet and simply feel their presence."

I sat on a rock adjacent to the path and closed my eyes to see if I could sense what he was talking about. Almost immediately a tingle in my stomach forced an uncontrollable laugh.

"Yes, they're quite playful. And they sure are curious about you! Do you feel that?"

"Um, I think so." I did feel something strange, and *playful* was definitely a good word to describe it. As I opened my eyes, I saw a bright blue dragonfly hovering a few inches in front of my nose, as if to stare directly into my eyes. It sped off as quickly as it had arrived, and then I saw four more, following a triangle path above my head. Within seconds they seemed to multiply into dozens, and less than a minute later there were literally hundreds of dragonflies all darting in between the trees, following the same triangular pattern. One at a time, they would hover within inches of my nose until I began to get dizzy.

"Dragonflies!" I was nearly speechless as my heart raced with excitement. I had always been attracted to these graceful creatures, but I had never seen so many in one place.

"Yes, fairy spirits take the form of dragonflies when they want humans to see them. Aren't they beautiful?"

"There are so many! What are they doing here?"

"Every tree in the forest has a nature spirit to look out for it, and since we're in the mountains, there are lots of tree fairies to take care of them. Everyone has a job to do on this planet, and that's theirs. They are lucky: they are born knowing what their destiny is. It's harder for humans, since the first part of their journey is discovering what they are meant to do."

After a few hours it began to darken under the tree-lined canopy above the meadow, and the light began to play hide-and-seek with the shadows. The greens and blues turned to browns and purples, and faces in the tree bark emerged and retreated with every second. The dragonflies flew away to their respective tree houses, and Robert collected Puppy Don, who was fast asleep in the grassy meadow.

Robert quietly gestured for me to follow him, and we made our way to the other side of the meadow, which was still illuminated by twilight. We then came upon a large irrigation ditch with a well-worn walking path along its grassy lip. I could hear that a stream was still flowing even though it was summer, and I was comforted by the soothing water sounds that caressed the rocks and pebbles on its journey through the forest.

"Watch your step," Robert said as we transitioned onto the side of the culvert. "I have something very special to show you."

We followed the stream for about ten minutes until we came to an open field just as the night had fully committed to darkness.

"Look at that!" he exclaimed while pointing at the large moon peeking from behind the mountains across the valley. We both sat down in the clearing and watched the silvery moon ascend to illuminate the darkened sky. The moonrise was breathtaking, and I couldn't remember if I had ever taken the time to *really* watch it before.

As soon as the silvery orb had fully revealed itself, Robert said, "This is a very special full moon tonight. It's called the Blessing Moon, and it represents the union of the earth and sky. It is traditionally a time to *begin* a spiritual journey, as the power of summer fills nature with fullness and abundance."

"Are you ready?" he asked.

"Ready for what?"

"Ready to breathe in the energy of the moon?"

"What does that mean?"

He ignored my question and proceeded to guide me through a series of actions that I reluctantly followed. "First, stand up and bend your knees slightly. Then bend your elbows so your upper arms are perpendicular to your forearms, and raise your hands up on either side of your head with your palms open, facing the moon."

Robert contorted himself while talking, and I mirrored his movements the best I could.

"Good," he continued. "Now lift your head back so your nostrils are aligned with the moon. And squint your eyes so you're looking at it through your eyelashes."

It wasn't the most comfortable position in the world, and my neck and lower back started to ache almost immediately.

"Now breathe in the energy of the moon through your nostrils in long, slow, deep breaths. Hold the energy inside of you for a count of five, and then slowly exhale through your mouth."

I followed his lead, and after a while I thought I could feel the lunar energy enter my nostrils, travel down my throat, and accumulate in the pit of my stomach. It was a cool, calming feeling; and the more I consumed, the more I felt a reservoir of energy fill my insides. However, my excitement was quickly replaced by a cramping pain in my neck and lower back, and after just a few minutes I had to sit down.

When I glanced over to Robert, I saw that he had placed his right foot on the inside of his left thigh just above the knee and was balancing on one leg. Without moving a muscle he said, "Don't worry—it takes time for your body to feel comfortable in that position. Even a few deep breaths will give you enough energy to last until the next full moon. I try to breathe in every full moon to give me strength for the month."

I could see why he would do this regularly and thought that I should try it myself. I felt more powerful than I ever had, and the moon energy felt like it was waiting for me to call on it whenever I needed extra help.

"The lunar energy in the mountains is much more powerful than in most other places," he said after a long silence. "The only other place on Earth that has access to really powerful moon energy is in the heart of the desert."

Robert lowered his leg and opened his bag, which was on the ground next to Puppy Don. He pulled out a small bracelet and handed it to me with both hands while bowing his head. It had several round orange gemstones with silver discs that were sandwiched between white opal-like stones that glimmered in the moonlight.

"I made this for you. It has carnelian to help you speak your truth, moonstone to nurture your intuition, and silver moons to help retain the lunar energy you received tonight. Wear it every day for the next twenty-eight days and you will begin to feel its power. The power of gemstones is one of nature's gifts. There are many moons of energy already contained in these stones, and you can bring it with you during the daylight hours. However, it's important to keep the bracelet charged by putting it outside in a dish of saltwater every full moon."

"I will," I said as I fastened the bracelet onto my wrist. I'd never worn jewelry before, but for some reason this bracelet felt like it was already a part of me. It was like a long-lost friend that had just found its way back to my wrist.

After a few more minutes, Robert looked up at the sky and said, "I have to go." He gathered his belongings and picked up Puppy Don, who was still sleeping. "I have a lot to do tonight, and I completely lost track of time. Stay here as long as you want—do you know your way back?"

"I think so, but I'm done." I was starting to get cold, and I was just wearing short sleeves. I hadn't expected to be gone past dark.

"Okay, let's go."

We retraced our steps along the grassy lip of the winding culvert, and the water below reflected the silvery light of the moon. When we finally returned to the meadow, it looked and sounded much different than I remembered. It was as if someone had rearranged all the fallen trees along the path and blotted out key rays of moonlight to deliberately confuse any visitors. I was sure I would have lost my way if I'd been alone.

As we walked, Robert continued to answer my questions.

"How can the full moon give you energy?" I asked.

"It's simple. Everything in the universe is merely an exchange of energy. It either helps collect energy or it helps expend energy. The Chinese have called this yin and yang. I assume you are familiar with the yin-yang symbol?"

"Of course. The black-and-white circle thingy."

"Exactly. Moonlight is filled with yin energy, which is restorative. And during the full moon, the yin energy is at its peak, so it's much easier to receive and store for later use. On the other side, the sun is filled with yang energy, which gives you the power to express yourself if you have yin energy in reserve. Does that make sense?"

"You mean, the moon fills up your bank account, and the sun helps spend it."

"That's a good way to describe it," he laughed. "What I wanted to show you is that nature can provide you with all the energy you need if you just slow down and let it help you. The moon, the sun, and everything else in nature has been provided by the universe to help us with our earthly needs. Unfortunately, over the past few hundred years, humans have been taught to ignore nature instead of turning to it for help—which is probably at the root of the reason the environment is in the shape it's in."

I didn't like to think about environmental issues at all because they were so depressing. And they seemed too big for me to do anything about.

Robert continued and seemed to address my concerns: "Not everyone has to be an activist to make a difference. Just doing what we did tonight can make a huge impact by our becoming part of the cycle of nature and reclaiming what has been ignored. Nature is a living, breathing thing, which is no different from you or me. When we feel loved, we have more energy to heal ourselves when sick. And when we're feeling ignored or unloved, we find it harder to recover from whatever ails us. By celebrating nature's cycles, we show it our love and it can begin to heal itself. It's not the only thing that needs to be done, but it's something we can all do as part of our everyday lives. And with the power of billions of souls on this planet, a massive healing can be done in a relatively short time."

I wasn't convinced that we could solve all the world's problems by simply celebrating nature's cycles. But I could definitely feel the energy of the moon inside me and thought that if it made *me* feel that good, I could probably make another living thing feel good if I tried. I filed that under

"It couldn't hurt" and vowed to spend a couple minutes every day sending the planet good wishes.

By then we had found our way down the hill and were approaching the town center.

"See you later," Robert said once we reached the bottom of the hill.

"When?" I asked, and instantly felt self-conscious about appearing needy.

"When the moment is right. We now have a connection that doesn't need to rely on archaic measurements of time. When the universe wants us to meet, then we'll meet."

Robert waved goodbye and headed out of town while I walked in the opposite direction toward my apartment. My thoughts were swimming with everything that had happened that day, and I was completely exhausted when I finally arrived at my front door. After climbing into bed and letting myself sink into the silence around me, I was able to feel the moon energy even more so than I had outside. It was still bubbling in the pit of my stomach, and with a smile on my lips, I quickly drifted off to sleep.

CHAPTER THREE

woke up throughout the night and wasn't able to sleep well because of my recurring nightmare. Several years prior, I had been engaged to a girl named Cheryl, and we were to marry in the spring. We'd originally met in high school but didn't begin dating until we left and found ourselves living in the nearby town of Yreka. After rediscovering each other, we had an instant connection, and I always felt lucky to have found true love at such an early age.

Cheryl was short with curly black hair, and had a knack for the culinary arts and making me laugh. After graduating from high school, she immediately found a job as a sous-chef in a popular restaurant that was favored by the tourists in a nearby town. She became quite successful in a short amount of time and began moonlighting at night to get her own catering business off the ground. On occasion I helped her with the bookkeeping and serving clients during events, and it was our dream to eventually work together full-time once the business could support us.

One of the most prestigious catering jobs we landed was a lawyers' convention at a mountain retreat. It was easily the biggest event we had ever catered, and it was going to give us enough money so that Cheryl could quit her day job and work on the catering business full-time. When the event was less than a week away, I began to get a really bad feeling about it and tried desperately to get her to cancel. Doing so wasn't practical, as the food had already been ordered, and Cheryl was worried that our reputation would be ruined because the lawyers were so connected. The feeling was so strong that I couldn't let it rest, and eventually stopped helping her prepare. We fought about it night and day, and by the time the event came around, we weren't talking to each other and I refused to go.

On the way back from the event around 3 A.M., Cheryl was driving through the mountains and a drunk driver swerved into her lane and hit her head-on. She was killed instantly.

Unfortunately, that's not the dream. That part is real.

In the dream, Cheryl pulls herself from the wreckage, her face marred with scratches and her arms covered in blood. Her outstretched hands are cupped in an offering while she slowly walks toward me. She tries to give me something, but I won't allow myself to look at it because whatever she's carrying absolutely terrifies me. There are other people in the dream watching and waiting for my reaction, including my mother, who's holding a baby; a policeman; and a girl from high school who had also been killed in a car accident. As soon as Cheryl gets close enough to touch, I turn from her and run away. That's when I wake up, my heart pounding and the sheets drenched in cold sweat.

I had dreamt the same exact dream nearly every night since she died. Evidently I was going to be haunted for the rest of my life, which served me right for not going with her that fatal night. I was positive that I could have done something to help her avoid the drunk driver if I hadn't been so headstrong and had agreed to go. Perhaps she was distracted with the radio and I could have watched the road, or maybe I would have swerved differently if I had been driving . . .

CHAPTER FOUR

My new apartment was definitely at the upper end of my budget, and as the days progressed, I began to get nervous about money. I still hadn't discovered all the potential employers in Ashland, but it looked like the big options were the Shakespeare theater, the university, or restaurants and shops that offered service-type jobs. I didn't have any qualifications to work at a university or a theater, so I systematically went through the phone book and called all the shops and restaurants. I knew that I wouldn't make the same money I had in L.A., but I decided that it was better to adjust my lifestyle so I could live in a town I actually liked.

However, nearly all the conversations went the same way:

"Hello, I'm looking for work. May I drop off my résumé?"

"Sorry, we're completely staffed at the moment, but you can check back after summer."

An exceptionally gregarious woman who worked at the Native American shop explained further, putting my insecurities to rest: "All the college students fill in during the summer, which is perfect for the tourist season. But once school starts in the fall, we'll be looking for help from people who don't need a flexible schedule."

I had saved enough money to keep me going through the next season, so I decided to look upon this as an opportunity to enjoy the summer without responsibilities and resume my job search in the fall. It would give me enough time to really explore what Ashland was all about and get to know myself again. I'd always spent most of my time working and hadn't taken a summer off since high school. And although I was still nervous about money, I was secretly excited about what I would discover without the responsibility of a job.

I began getting strong feelings to meet up with Robert again, and I remembered what he'd said about knowing when the time was right. I wasn't sure where to find him, but it seemed reasonable to return to the place where we'd originally met. As I approached the Co-op, I barely recognized him, since he was wearing a brightly colored poncho-like shirt and loose-fitting cream-colored pants. I was relieved to discover that he had more than one change of clothes, although the South American hippie garb was a bit off-putting. As I got closer, I could see that he was talking to a young dread-locked mother wearing a tie-dyed skirt who was pushing an infant in a spoke-wheeled stroller that read: "Powered by Bio-Diesel."

"I offer my humble gratitude to you for sharing your unique light with the world. You are truly blessed," she said in a high-pitched, airy voice as she dropped a dollar onto the blanket Puppy Don was lying on. She waved goodbye and wheeled her child down the concrete ramp and along the opposite sidewalk from where I was approaching.

"You seem like you're in a good mood," I commented after the hippie chick left.

"It's been a good day," Robert said as he gathered the handful of crumpled bills and coins that surrounded the sleeping puppy. "Too bad the wind picked up earlier," he chuckled. "I lost nearly half of the loot."

"Why do you just leave it lying around? Shouldn't you put it in a safer place?" For being so smart in some ways, he seemed remarkably dim in others.

"It's not for me to decide who needs the money," he said, his tone becoming quite serious. "It's only my job to collect it. The wind will spend it on those who need it most. And besides, I'm always left with as much as I need. It's best to only eat when hungry."

As I let his curious words sink in, I reflected on the cardboard sign leaning against the tree that had previously kept Robert upright:

Remember the womb.

I wondered how I'd known I was hungry when I was in the womb. I was always careful about what I ate, but it had been a constant struggle as long as I could remember. And ever since I had moved to image-conscious Los Angeles, I'd weighed myself nearly every day to make sure the calories weren't going to the wrong place. But in the womb I'd presumably had as much as I could eat twenty-four hours a day for nine months, and weighing in at six pounds one ounce at birth, I didn't seem to have any problems with overeating back then.

"Come with me," said Robert as he put Puppy Don in a front-loading baby carrier before starting to walk up 1st Street. The sun retreated behind the clouds that had been gathering all morning, and the temperature instantly dropped a few degrees, which was a welcome change from the heat wave that had been lingering since I arrived. This time I was prepared for hiking—I brought my own bottle of water, wore my hiking shoes with extra-thick socks, and tied a long-sleeved flannel overshirt around my waist in case we were going to be out after dark.

Puppy Don woke up briefly as Robert slid him into the canvas sling, and he eyed me through half-awake slits. But after a few steps, he quickly returned to his puppy slumber.

"Today is a very special day for you," Robert said after we were a few blocks from the Co-op. "We're going to find something of yours that has been lost."

"Something of mine that has been lost? What have I lost?"

"You have lost a piece of your soul. And a very large one at that."

"I lost my soul? When did I lose it?" I asked.

"I don't know for sure, but I'm guessing it was many seasons ago."

We walked on the sidewalk next to a cemetery for a few blocks and turned left onto the street that led to the freeway. The charm of downtown Ashland dissipated quickly as we approached the outskirts, and by the time we neared the freeway, it was all but gone. It would have looked like any other suburban American crossroads if it wasn't for the surrounding forest and mountains.

"How can you tell that I lost a piece of my soul?"

"Because it has a big black hole in it. That's the first thing I noticed at the Co-op when you rejected my gift."

"I was hoping you didn't recognize that that was me," I said sheepishly while once again trying to figure out exactly what gift he had offered.

"How could I *not* recognize you? You're walking around with a large hole in your soul. Anyone can see it if they just look."

That made me feel instantly self-conscious. I'd always taken the time to make sure my clothes were clean, wrinkle free, and all matching; and then I found out I had a big black hole in my soul that anyone could see.

"Don't worry about it—most people don't look." Robert always seemed to know what I was thinking. "They're so busy worrying about the physical that they seldom pay attention to the spiritual. Lucky for you, too, because your spiritual side is quite a mess."

I wasn't sure if that made me feel any better. "So you really think we can find my missing soul today?"

"I don't know if we'll find all of it today, but I do know we'll get started. I have a hunch you already know where to look for the first piece."

That got me thinking: *Where would I have lost it? How is it possible to lose a soul in the first place?* When we crossed the freeway, I began to imagine that I could feel the edges of my soul. As I traced them, I noticed an area that didn't feel as alive as the rest. It felt remarkably like a callous—healed over and devoid of any feeling. Was I a freak? Simply clumsy? Or forgetful? How many people were walking around leaving pieces of their souls around? And what happened to them when they were lost? Did souls go bad? I had a million questions but wasn't sure how to pose them.

"What part of my soul is missing?" I finally asked.

"I'm not sure, but we'll find out soon."

We turned onto Dead Indian Memorial Road, which struck me as an ominous name for a lonely road on the outskirts of town. As I looked around, I noticed that the landscape was colored in markedly different hues than those of the town center. The hills above Ashland were painted with the vibrant colors of leaves and flowers, while the valley below was carpeted with low-growing pale yellow grasses. Even the dirt seemed drier, and with every step, my mouth lost its moisture and my lips began to crack. I was thankful that I had brought my own bottle of water, and I kept the cap unscrewed so I could continue to sip as we walked even deeper into the country.

Eventually we came to a painted metal gate chained to a thick cedar post, which Robert opened just wide enough for me to squeeze through. The dirt road was no longer maintained, and we made our way through the tall, deadened grasses, where dozens of grasshoppers bounced arclike to avoid our every step. Over the third hill we came to a pointed white tipi sunk into the middle of the golden field. I had never seen a tipi up close before, and the conical structure—made from ripped white canvas and weathered wooden poles sticking out the top—was much larger than I would have imagined.

"Here we are," Robert said proudly as he gestured to the tipi.

"Is that yours?"

"Yes," he replied as he unhitched Puppy Don from his chest and placed him on the ground. "Come on in." Robert untied the entry flaps under six horizontal wooden sutures sewn into the fabric, and I followed both of them through the womblike opening. Once inside, the puppy stretched briefly, sauntered over to a folded pad of fur-covered blankets, and immediately curled up and returned to the business of napping.

"He sure sleeps a lot," I noticed.

"You would, too, if you just returned from the dead. It takes a lot out of you."

"Oh."

The inside of the tipi reeked of smoke, and the hazy darkness was cut by a single shaft of light that fell immediately to the right of Puppy Don. There were stacks of clothes, bulging paper bags, and several Native American wool blankets around the perimeter of the dirt-floored circular room. In the center was a sunken fire pit within an intricately arranged circle of large stones, and a blackened iron teapot was suspended by a trio of branches tied together with baling wire. Robert unfolded one of the handmade blankets in the center of the spotlight and gestured for me to sit down. As I made myself comfortable, he lit a small fire in the center pit and unwrapped four leather pouches filled with freshly cut herbs.

"This morning I gathered medicine from the surrounding fields that should help you."

"Medicine? What kind of medicine?"

"Plant medicine. It will calm you down so you can travel with me to the past and retrieve your soul."

The teapot began to steam, and a few minutes later, whistled to indicate that it was ready. Robert grabbed an irregularly shaped turquoise ceramic cup from one of the paper sacks, and inside he dropped two pinches of each of the herbs he had prepared. As he poured in the steaming liquid, the tipi filled with a powerful scent that was as unusual as it was familiar.

"Here, drink this," he said as he handed me the cup of herbal medicine.

I cupped the glazed ceramic vessel with both hands and brought it to my nose and inhaled. The grassy fragrance was sweet and dusty, not unlike the warm summer day outside, and it had a musty hint of what could most easily be described as dirt. I cautiously sipped the warm brew, and although it was unlike any tea I'd had before, it was surprisingly tasty.

"I'm not going to start hallucinating, am I?"

"Not from the tea," Robert laughed.

The liquid began to calm my nerves, and I tried to let myself relax and enjoy the experience I was having. I was both excited and nervous about what would happen next, but I trusted Robert and believed that he had my best interest at heart.

After making sure I was comfortable and giving me a second blanket in case I needed it, he lit dried herbs in four ceramic dishes and let the smoldering leaves fill the tipi with smoke. I recognized the aroma of sage and cedar, but I hadn't smelled the other herbs before.

Robert then picked up a shallow handmade drum and began beating it slowly and deliberately. The large instrument was made from two white leather skins stretched across a hollowed wooden stump and fastened together with yellowed leather strips in a crisscrossed pattern. There was also a single gray speckled feather tied to the drum that danced with every strike of his hand-carved wooden mallet.

"Okay, now we're ready. Finish the medicine and lie down on your back."

I drank the tea, handed him the empty container, and stretched out fully on the wool blanket after propping the back of my head up with the second blanket.

"Close your eyes and let the sunbeam warm your face."

I closed my eyes and smiled as the warm sunlight caressed my cheeks. My head pulsed in time with the drum as Robert began to strike it at faster intervals.

"I have surrounded this tipi with white light, and today we call on the elders to help find and retrieve the missing pieces of Scott's soul so he can be whole again. Please help us journey through the past, the future, and all the places that Scott has been or will ever be in this lifetime. And help us find the pieces of his lost soul that are ready to rejoin Scott's present path."

Robert's breathing quickened and filled the spaces between the drumbeats with the sound of wind.

After several minutes, he finally spoke. "Your power animal has taken the form of a raven, and it has led me to a young woman in a car who has a piece of your soul. She is no longer of this world, but she has not yet journeyed to the other side."

I immediately got chills over my entire body and tried to wrap myself in the blanket I was lying on.

"Do you know who this is?"

"Uh-huh." I was barely able to choke back the tears. "Cheryl."

"Good. Cheryl wants you to know that she is okay, and she wishes you well. But it is time for her to leave, and you need to accept your soul back so she can continue on her journey."

I started to feel guilty. Was I somehow preventing Cheryl from moving on to the other side?

The drumming became more and more intense, and I thought I heard Puppy Don whimper in the corner.

"Scott, are you ready to receive the missing piece of your soul?"

"Yes." I was barely able to use my voice, as I could sense something big was about to happen.

"I ask for the support and strength of the sacred raven, representing intuition and spiritual awakening. Please help us retrieve Scott's soul from Cheryl and bring it safely and purposefully back to this dimension, where it may reside with its rightful owner."

At almost that exact moment, the sun darkened outside and the air in the tipi became freezing cold. It went from summer to winter in a matter of seconds, and the fire in the center was extinguished without ceremony. The smoke from the herbs began to tickle the back of my throat, and the insistent drumming made my temples throb in time.

"Scott, open your palms to the sky and prepare to receive what is yours."

"Okay," I said, hoping that I was doing it right.

"Is your heart open and filled with love?"

"Yes," I whispered. I concentrated on my love for Cheryl and intuitively pressed my chest outward as far as it would go.

Robert started chanting something I couldn't understand, and I began to feel nauseated while the bottoms of my feet tingled. The feeling moved up the back of my legs to the base of my spine and eventually found its way to the back of my neck. The drumming continued to increase in intensity until all of a sudden it stopped, and silence fell over the tipi with the heaviness of a large wool blanket.

I opened my eyes and could barely see through the darkness, but as my eyes adjusted, I was able to make out Robert, who was lighting a long, narrow pipe with a smoldering branch from the extinguished fire.

"The raven has returned with the missing piece of your soul and is among us now. I will now breathe in what has been retrieved, and as I exhale, you will receive what is yours."

Robert placed his lips on the narrow shaft of the pipe and inhaled fully, deep into his lungs. He gently put the pipe down on the ground with both hands and then cupped them in the same way Cheryl had done in my dreams. He closed his eyes and blew the smoke out of his mouth, through his cupped hands, and onto my chest. At precisely the same moment, the wind blew through the untied canvas panels at the top of the tipi and filled the air with the sound of flapping wings.

The smoke felt like it effortlessly permeated my skin and seeped directly into my internal organs. It instantly warmed my insides and quickly began to spread—first to my lungs, then to my heart, then to my stomach, and then throughout my neck and limbs. I felt a wave of emotion unlike any I had ever experienced before, and I immediately started to weep. The smoke filled me with sadness and I couldn't control my tears. I was literally convulsing with sorrow as tears flowed for what seemed to be hours. I couldn't speak. I couldn't think. All I could do was *feel* . . . feel sadness and grief.

"Welcome your soul back to you. Let it know how glad you are to have it again, and promise you will take good care of it and will never let it go."

I tried my best to follow his instructions, but all I could do was cry.

"You gave Cheryl a piece of your soul, which you believed was the ultimate gift, but nobody can use your soul other than you yourself."

My reintegrated soul was swirling inside, and I could actually feel the new part of me that had returned like an old friend. It was tender and felt exposed to the elements when I moved. Gradually my vision began to blur, and I felt as if I were falling deep into the earth while losing my grasp on consciousness.

"Close your eyes," Robert said kindly. "It's time for you to rest."

I followed his advice . . . and surrendered to a deep, deep sleep.

CHAPTER FIVE

When I awoke the next morning, I could almost taste the stale smoke that permeated my clothes. As I opened my eyes and saw the pointed peak of the canvas tipi, it took me a moment to remember where I was and what I'd been doing. After I reclaimed my faculties, I rolled over, expecting to find Robert and Puppy Don, but they were nowhere to be seen. There were several blankets and items of clothing strewn across the dirt floor, and the center pit was no longer smoldering from the previous night's fire.

I emerged from the tipi and called out to my friends, but they were obviously long gone. After the muted light inside of the tipi, the sun nearly blinded me when I was outside. The light seemed to scream at me, and I covered my eyes for a few seconds until they adjusted. When I was able to focus, all of the colors seemed much brighter and all the sounds were much louder. It was as if the volume on everything was turned up, and I could see and hear clearly for the first time in my life. I spun around in place and was taken by the beauty of the valley I was in. The dried grasses became beautiful golden strands bending in the breeze, and the mountains were proud protectors of the valley below. It was as if I were seeing pure beauty for the first time in my life, and it was alive. The energy of beauty emanated from every living thing around me, and I was in awe.

Then almost immediately I imagined it all disappearing into nothingness. My heart sank as I realized that Cheryl was gone forever, and I dropped to my knees and began to sob. I couldn't control my emotions, and I kept moving from extreme elation to deep sadness from one minute to the next. I could feel my emotions much more deeply than I ever had before, and since I hadn't previously let go of Cheryl, her death seemed to hit me all at once.

I entered the tipi one last time to gather my overshirt and make sure I hadn't left anything behind, and then followed the lightly worn path across the grassy fields toward town. When I first saw houses, mailboxes, and cars again, it was a shock—I was surprised by how quickly I'd become used to being surrounded by nothing but nature.

As I walked toward town, I reflected on what had happened the day before and traced the edges of the hole I had felt in my soul. I was pleased to discover that it was mostly filled in. The piece of me that had previously been dead was now very much alive and adjusting to the outside world, but was still quite sensitive and fragile.

I hadn't had anything to eat since the previous morning and decided to stop by my favorite sandwich place once I arrived back in town. When I entered the restaurant, the contrast to the outdoors was quite dramatic—not only in the lighting and the smells, but in the feeling. When I was outside, it felt light and airy; but once inside, I felt a muddled energy that weighed on my heart. It also didn't help that every square inch of the walls was covered floor to ceiling with framed black-and-white photos and wicker-basket sculptures of everything from farm animals to airplanes. The cluttered wall coverings made me feel claustrophobic compared to the simple canvas walls of the tipi, and I probably would have left if I hadn't been so hungry.

I found an available table at the front of the restaurant and placed my order with the short, tattooed waitress with a raspy voice. She wore her dyed red hair in a makeshift bun, and her clumpy mascara implied a late night out that she still hadn't recovered from. While I was waiting for the food to arrive, I could feel a huge dark cloud coming from the back kitchen that slowly began to fill the entire restaurant. And as I was sitting on the black vinyl seat, I discovered that I could feel the emotions of each person there simply by being open to them. It was as if everyone's true feelings flowed to me like the ocean tides, and as the waves broke, I could sense their emotions as if they were my own. And although it was entertaining at first, most people in the restaurant weren't very happy, so I tried to ignore everyone as best I could.

When my food finally arrived, I was surprised to discover that there was also energy emanating from the sandwich on the plate. It was nearly identical to the dark cloud I felt coming from the back kitchen, and I became quite agitated when I picked the sandwich up. I wasn't sure what was happening to me, but I knew that I was hungry and had to eat. I decided to put the sandwich down, and bit into one of the cut carrots garnishing the plate. They were still fresh, and I could feel the life force entwine with mine as I chewed, swallowed, and felt it make its way down my throat. The pieces of carrot were definitely satisfying, but unfortunately there were only three. All that was left after I ate them was the turkey-and-Swiss I had ordered, and when I picked it up, I again felt the dark energy begin to agitate me. The sandwich looked great, but when I bit into it, I almost choked. I felt as if I'd consumed someone else's anger with that first bite, and it was toxic to me.

I couldn't help myself from spitting the mouthful onto the plate, and I rubbed my eyes while trying to figure out what was happening to me. My stomach was threatening to empty, and my head was swirling as if I were going to pass out. I pushed the plate to the opposite end of the table, which helped a bit, but I was still quite dizzy. I had completely lost my appetite and didn't want to remain there any longer. And as I looked around the restaurant, I could sense that the energy from all the patrons was becoming even darker than it had been before. It was as if they'd all come there to consume the chef's anger and were filling themselves up with it, whether they wanted to or not.

I clumsily tossed some crumpled bills on the table and quickly left the restaurant. Outside, I gradually felt much better as the wave of nausea began to dissipate in the fresh air. Something about the soul retrieval had made me ultrasensitive to other people's energy, and I was surprised by how profound the sensitivity was. I was also genuinely upset about the horrible experience I'd had in the restaurant. Letting the chef transfer his bad energy into the food of others was inexcusable. According to the sign on the door, the restaurant prided itself on using only the freshest organic ingredients, but the food was completely ruined by the chef's mood.

I decided to take it easy and relax for the rest of the day. I made my way to the entrance of Lithia Park and strolled through the initial lawn adjacent to downtown. I'd been there a few times before, but it was like I was seeing everything for the first time. Throughout the park, exotic plants were labeled with brass name tags, and the paths were groomed with a luxurious layer of wood chips that felt soft to the feet. And the babbling creek flowed through the park, carrying its soothing sounds over the pebbled banks.

The park was unusually tranquil, and I spent the rest of the day exploring—lazing in different corners, determined to find the ideal spot. Just above the upper duck pond I finally found a warm patch of grass by the creek that seemed to have my name on it. Lying down on nature's green blanket, I felt a gentle breeze caress my face while I listened to the peaceful water sounds of the creek flowing nearby. For the first time since my childhood, I fell asleep under the clouds and drifted in and out of consciousness for what seemed to be hours. I was still deeply saddened by the memory of Cheryl, but the natural beauty of the park was rejuvenating, and I felt purified as the afternoon progressed.

As the sun went down, I made my way back to the Co-op to pick up some prepared brown rice to satisfy my returning hunger before I made my way home. I was disappointed that Robert and Puppy Don weren't there, and I began to feel abandoned by them. After such an intense experience, I felt that I really needed to talk to somebody who understood what I was going through, and wondered why Robert had left without even saying goodbye. And the more I thought about it, the more angry I became. He was directly responsible for everything I was going through, and I felt like he had deserted me without any explanation.

Perhaps I was feeling overemotional, but I was still angry at him when I finally made it back to my apartment. After drinking several tall glasses of water and eating a few bites of brown rice, I crawled into my soft bed and cocooned myself tightly within my blankets so that I couldn't see or feel anything else from the outside world.

CHAPTER SIX

The next morning I was awakened by a knock on my door, and when I unlatched the lock, I saw a short woman with long wavy blonde hair wearing a flowing white dress. She had kind eyes and a Mona Lisa smile that exuded a contentment I recognized but seldom felt myself. Maybe I was still lingering in dreamland, but it also looked like she didn't have any edges separating her body from the surroundings.

"Scott?" she asked.

"Uh-huh," I replied while still rubbing the sleep from my eyes.

"Hi, I'm Martika. Robert told me you had some very intense work done, and you brought back a pretty significant piece of your soul."

"You know Robert?"

She nodded.

"Where is he?" My anger began to return. "He just left me without even saying goodbye."

"He does that sometimes." She nodded sympathetically. "I know he's very busy at the moment, but he *does* need to work on his bedside manner."

"How did you know where to find me?" I was starting to wake up, and I began to get a strange feeling about what was happening. "I never told Robert where I lived."

"It's a small town," she laughed. "Everyone knows everyone's business—you will soon enough. My friend Leslie rented this apartment to you. She told me about you when you first came to town. My daughter also used to live here. It has a lovely view from the bedroom, don't you think?"

I nodded as I remembered Leslie the landlord with her silver SUV. Thinking back, I remembered she did seem to be awfully chatty about the neighbors, and I made a mental note to be extra careful about what I said in this town.

"Can I come in?" Martika asked.

"Oh yes, sorry. I'm kind of out of it at the moment."

"No problem," she said as I shut the door behind her. After we sat down on my brown and black sectional, she appeared to gradually come into focus, although her lips didn't seem to move very much when she spoke.

"How does your soul feel?" she asked in a concerned voice after arranging a large pillow to support her back.

That was a good question. I finally said, "It feels tender."

"Yes, *tender* is a good word. I've done a lot of soul retrieval, and the reclaimed soul always feels tender after reintegration. Now is a very special time—it's important to give it attention and gratitude for returning so that it can adapt gracefully."

I nodded.

"And how is your mood?" she continued.

I felt as if I'd been crying for days, and I was still quite melancholy. I had never let myself grieve for the death of Cheryl, and years of sorrow were hitting me all at once. "I'm very sad," I said after a long pause.

"That's because you lost someone very dear to you, and you weren't able to process your grief because your soul was in shock when you lost her. Robert and I both think it's going to be very difficult for you to deal with this on your own, and we believe you need a support group to help you."

"Oh, I'm not sure I need *that*." I dreaded the idea of a fluorescent-lit office building filled with bad coffee, stale doughnuts, and depressed people.

"It's not what you think," Martika continued. "You've cut yourself off from your ancestors, and they are willing to help you through all this. But you need to get in touch with them, and the easiest way is with a constellation."

"What's that?"

"A constellation allows you to reach out to your family soul, which gives you the power to live your daily life with the support of your ancestors. You have recently reclaimed your personal soul, but it carries too much weight for you to shoulder on your own. That's why you couldn't handle the death of Cheryl. Every one of us has access to our family soul, which is like an unconditional support system."

I had no idea what she was talking about. I'd just gone through an intense experience getting a missing piece of my own soul back. Now I was told I needed to get my *family* soul back, which was something I didn't even know I had. I was filled with sadness, but I was also starting to get angry. Who was this person, and why was she coming after me like this? I just wanted to sleep. I was so tired. Why couldn't she just let me sleep?!

"Come on, Scott—it'll be good for you. There's a constellation starting in an hour, and I think you should go."

I really didn't want to go anywhere, but I didn't have the energy to protest. I was still a little shaky, so Martika helped me down the weathered wooden steps and into her white Subaru station wagon. It was the first time I'd been in a car since mine had died, and it felt unusually confining.

We followed the main road to the southernmost edge of town and veered away from Dead Indian Memorial toward Mount Ashland. When we were nearly to the town limits, we turned off the main road and drove through a neighborhood filled with manicured country estates. Acres of white picket fences contained fields of livestock, including horses, sheep, llamas, and goats. After about a mile and a half, Martika pulled into a pea-graveled driveway between two imposing red barnlike buildings that marked the entry to a large country-style compound. We slowly drove up the circular driveway and parked near a small white round building with a wood-shingle roof that was partially shaded by a pair of majestic oaks.

"Here we are," said Martika. "Stay in the car for a moment and I'll get everything ready for you."

There were several people milling about the smaller building, and I again became acutely aware of the stench of smoke on my clothes. I was so tired from the previous night that I still hadn't taken a shower since I'd spent the night in the tipi. And in my groggy state, I had put on the same clothes I'd been wearing the day before. I began to feel very uncomfortable and wondered if there was time to clean up before the constellation began.

Martika appeared a couple of minutes later and said, "They're ready for you. Come on, let's go in."

At that instant, I was inexplicably terrified of the constellation session. "Maybe today isn't the right day for me." I tried to think of a good excuse to leave.

"It'll be okay—I'll be with you the whole time. There's nothing to be worried about."

Although I had just met Martika, I wanted to believe her because she seemed genuinely filled with love and kindness. I was still feeling ultra-emotional from the soul retrieval, and I didn't really want to be alone. It was nice to be cared for again after so many years.

"Come on," she said and led me by the hand into the small building.

The interior was both elegant and dramatic. It had a round, open floor plan, with a huge fireplace and knotted-wood panels on the ceiling, which featured a brightly painted Native American cross-like symbol carved into its peak. Resting on the dark honey wood floor were several boxes of tissue, and chairs were arranged in a circle around the perimeter of the room. About fifteen women and two men were seated in the chairs, all wearing pale blue and white HELLO MY NAME IS tags. The tree-filtered light found its way in through the windows, and the room had the comforting aroma of fresh sawdust and orange blossom.

"This is Scott," announced Martika. "He just had some very intense soul-retrieval work done, and he needs our help."

"Hi, Scott," the group said in unison, and I instantly felt more awkward than I had since high school.

"And this is Hans." Martika gestured to a tall man with shoulder-length gray hair. "He'll be facilitating the constellation today.

scott blum

"Let's start with Scott," said Hans. "Please sit here next to me."

I tentatively sat down next to him while Martika's mouth shaped a smile as if to say that it would all be okay.

Hans continued, "Before we get started, I want everyone to open themselves up to the *field*. Breathe in through your nose, deep into your heart, and slowly breathe out through your mouth."

Everyone followed his instructions, and the room filled with the windlike sound of breath.

After a few minutes, Hans spoke directly to me: "What's on your heart today, Scott?"

I looked around and everyone's eyes were fixed on me. I didn't know what to say but finally uttered a single word: "Sadness."

"And why are you sad?"

"Because my fiancée was killed. And I feel alone."

"Uh-huh. What was your fiancée's name?"

"Cheryl."

"And how did she die?"

"She was killed by a drunk driver."

There were immediately sounds of pity that filled the room—sounds I was very familiar with, and the main reason I didn't usually talk about what happened to Cheryl.

"Okay, Scott, who in this room feels right to represent you?"

I didn't understand what he was asking. "Um, me, I guess . . ."

The room echoed with laughter, and I eyed the door to see if I could make a quick exit without anyone noticing.

"You can't be an active participant in the session; you have to sit outside the circle and watch once the constellation begins. Inside, the circle will transform into what we call the *field,* which is the gateway to our collective unconscious that connects us all through time and space. Use your intuition and pick someone who feels akin to the way you do right now."

I didn't understand everything he was saying, but I did realize that I was supposed to pick someone else to represent me during this exercise, whatever it was. I stood up and saw that there was only one other man in the group besides Hans. He had a black biker mustache and a large silver belt buckle. Definitely not someone I could relate to.

"It doesn't have to be a man." Hans seemed to read my mind. "Just pick someone who feels right."

I scanned the room and was immediately drawn to a girl in her midtwenties with short black hair, Goth makeup, and black clothes who was trying to avert her eyes so I wouldn't notice her. As I looked around, everyone else smudged together in a blur of color, while she remained in focus.

I slowly raised my hand and pointed while whispering to Hans, "Her."

"Lori, can you stand please?" he commanded.

"I'm representing Scott," Lori said as she walked into the circle.

"Good. Now who will represent Cheryl?"

I looked to the name tags, hoping I could find someone with a similar name to make it easier. The tags jumbled in a sea of letters, and I found myself overwhelmed and trembling. My legs nearly buckled under the weight of my torso, and I decided to sit down before it was too late.

"It's okay," said Hans. "Just pick the first person who feels right."

"Martika," I finally blurted out, hoping that she was still in the room. She was behind me arranging the buffet and walked toward Lori.

"I'm representing Cheryl," said Martika as she entered the circle.

"Very good," said Hans. "Let me help you with the rest. I would like to bring your grandfathers in to help. Are you okay with that?"

All of my grandfathers and great-grandfathers had passed away many years before. I had been closest with my grandfather on my mother's side, but I'd only seen him once every few years before his death. The others I hadn't really known very well. I didn't have much of an opinion one way or the other, and I heard myself say out loud, "Sure, if you think it would help." As I looked around, I could see a combination of sadness and compassion in nearly everyone's eyes as I spoke.

Hans continued with the determined precision of a cheetah stalking his prey: "Allie, you represent Scott's grandfather on his mother's side. Diana, you represent Scott's grandfather on his father's side. Shelley, you represent Scott's great-grandfather on his father's mother's side. Scott, what country is your great-grandfather from?"

It took a moment for me to figure out exactly *who* he was talking about, and after tracing an imaginary family tree with my index finger, I said, "He was Native American. Cherokee."

"I thought so. That makes a lot of sense. Devora, you represent the Cherokee nation. Hmm . . . that seems okay, but something's not in balance."

Hans tilted his head back and began to walk around in circles. From my vantage point, I couldn't see his face clearly, but it looked like his eyes rolled back into his head as he traced a figure-eight pattern with his large feet. This went on for several minutes, and I could tell that I wasn't the only one who was uncomfortable, as I began to see people shifting in their seats while waiting for him to finish.

Abruptly Hans stopped, and his eyes returned to center. He spoke with a commanding resonance that filled the entire room. "James," his voice echoed, "you represent the drunk driver who killed Cheryl."

Almost instantly, all of the blood in my entire body seemed to rush above my neck, and I could feel my face flush and turn red with anger as the "mustache" walked into the circle. I couldn't believe he was bringing *him* into the field. I tried getting up to leave, but Hans gently pushed me back into my seat and whispered something I didn't hear. I was absolutely livid. I wanted to get up and kick the drunk driver until he couldn't move. I was dizzy, and shaking so hard that the chair barely contained me.

Hans spoke up a bit louder: "Did the drunk driver survive?"

For some reason that took the edge off a bit. "No, he died also."

"We'll deal with that soon enough," Hans continued, "but now I want you to gently guide each of the helpers within the field to where they feel most natural. Just breathe into your heart and let the field guide you."

After taking a moment to recover, I deliberately walked over to Martika, and as I gently put my hands on the back of her shoulders, a tingly sensation flowed from her body, through my hands, up my arms, and down my spine. I let myself lean close enough to breathe in the scent of her hair and was immediately transported to the first time I'd met Cheryl. Martika became Cheryl with every passing moment—in her smell, her posture, and her aura. Within seconds, all of Martika's features were erased and only Cheryl remained.

"Just move her to where she feels most natural," Hans repeated.

Almost as if someone were pushing the back of my shoulders, I began to guide her to the far side of the circle, safe and away from the rest of the people.

"Good," said Hans. "Now the others."

I was similarly guided to move my own representative next to Cheryl so that they were standing side by side and gently facing each other. I looked at the rest of the group, and the only person I could see was the drunk driver. Anger returned and filled my heart when I looked at him. Without thinking, I pushed him to the opposite end of the circle from Cheryl and turned him around so he was facing toward the outside of it. If he had to be there, I wasn't going to let him be anywhere near Cheryl. He had done enough already, and he wasn't going to do any more if I could help it.

I looked at the rest of my family—my grand-fathers, my great-grandfather, and the Cherokee nation. I didn't feel a connection to any of them. Cheryl's death wasn't any of their business, and I couldn't understand why Hans had brought them here. I looked at Hans, shrugged my shoulders, and finally said, "I guess that's it." As I glanced back at Cheryl, I was shocked to find that I couldn't rec-ognize Martika at all. She had transformed into Cheryl and was looking right at me. The hairs on the back of my neck stood on end when I realized that it was the first time I had actually *seen* Cheryl in years.

"Okay, Scott, you're done for now. From here on out, I just need you to watch and feel. It's im-portant for you to stay quiet. Are you ready?"

I nodded my head, and the lights seemed to dim, although I didn't see anyone near the switch.

Hans walked up to my representative and asked, "How do you feel?"

"I feel angry at the drunk driver."

He then walked to the drunk driver and repeated his question: "How do you feel?"

"Shame. Regret," he said while starting to tear up. "I'm so sorry."

Hans continued, "I want you to say to Scott: 'I am sorry for taking Cheryl away from this world. It is my burden, and I alone will suffer the consequences.'"

Tears began to pool at the corners of his large mustache as the drunk driver repeated: "I am sorry for taking Cheryl away from this world. It is my burden, and I alone will suffer the consequences."

I watched dumbfounded, and I couldn't feel my feet anymore. I was completely numb inside and out and sensed that I was going into shock. My emotions felt like they'd begun to short-circuit. I didn't understand what was going on, but I knew I didn't like it.

Hans walked back to my representative and said, "Tell the drunk driver: 'I wronged you by taking on your burden. Cheryl's death is not my responsibility. It is your burden to carry.'"

My representative spoke slowly and clearly: "I wronged you by taking on your burden. Cheryl's death is not my responsibility. It is your burden to carry."

After a brief pause, Hans continued, "Tell him: 'I return your burden to you, and leave you in peace.'"

After an unusually long silence, my representative looked at me and then slowly returned her gaze to the drunk driver and whispered in a shaky voice, "I return your burden to you . . . and leave you in peace."

I put my head in my hands and began to sob uncontrollably. The soreness in my heart was replaced with a stabbing pain, and I couldn't stop crying. I was releasing years of anger that I'd previously inflicted on myself, and for the first time since Cheryl's death, I was able to release my burden. *It's not my fault.* I began to mouth the words over and over. *It's not my fault. It's not my fault. It's not my fault.*

The sobs of others surrounded me, and after my tears dried up, I felt like an emotional washrag that had just been wrung out. I instantly felt lighter as the guilt and anger in my heart began to dissipate. The constellation seemed to be working, and for the first time I was thankful to be there.

"Move at will," Hans commanded the group, which brought my focus back to the representatives in the circle.

Everyone in the group began to move toward one another in the center of the circle, without comforting my representative. Several attempted to avoid her altogether, while the others acted like they didn't see her, inevitably walking right into her, bumping her and literally spinning her around. Cheryl kept trying to get away from my representative, and every time my representative followed her, one of the others would run into her and nearly knock her down. This went on for almost three minutes and made me extremely uncomfortable.

"That's enough," Hans finally said. "Stop moving."

I was relieved and hoped it was finally over.

Hans weaved between each of the people in the field and stopped in front of my representative and asked, "What do you feel?"

"I feel alone. Like nobody wants to be with me," she replied.

Tears began streaming down my face again, and I couldn't keep my eyes open.

Through my emotional fog, I heard Hans continue: "That's because you are supposed to be dead. You were supposed to die with Cheryl."

I wasn't sure I had heard him right. He then repeated slowly and deliberately, *"That's because . . . you are supposed to be . . . dead. You were supposed to die with Cheryl."*

I had thought that a million times, but thought that people in Hans's position were obligated to make others feel good about living, not tell them they were supposed to be dead! I got really angry at him and wanted to get up and leave, but my legs wouldn't cooperate. In fact, my entire body wouldn't move. I was frozen there. Stilled, and forced to listen to his abuse.

"Usually destiny works hand in hand with free choice, but on occasion one can overtake the other, as it did in your case. Probably because you have a developed sense of intuition, you were able to sense that getting in the car didn't feel right." Hans continued, and his words began to come clear: "But the universe is a finely tuned machine, made up of billions of living things, all predetermined to move on a particular path, weaving in and out, without interfering with each other. When someone dies, traditionally that path is freed up for another living being to travel on."

My head started to spin again, and I wasn't sure I was following him anymore. He then looked directly at me and continued speaking: "In your case, the universe expects you to be dead, and the paths you are walking on are interfering with the paths from other souls' destinies. It's as if an old side road has continued to be used after a new freeway has been built right through it. It's very likely there will be run-ins because the side road is no longer supposed to be used."

I started to understand.

"That's why you feel so lonely, and why things have been so hard for you since Cheryl's passing."

I began to wonder if my recent string of bad luck had anything to do with what he was talking about. Before Cheryl's death, I would always find a parking space right in front of whatever store I was going to, I never had to wait in line for more than a few minutes, and I had great friends who would do anything for me. And it was true that after Cheryl's death, everything became much more difficult: I could never find any parking spaces, I would constantly be waiting in long lines for the simplest of things, and my friends nearly all abandoned me.

The more I thought about it, the more examples I came up with, like my recent habit of literally bumping into others when I was walking down the sidewalk. It was as if since Cheryl had died, most people couldn't even see that I existed. Even co-workers I would see every day had trouble remembering my name.

Hans explained, "It's also the reason why you've been holding on to Cheryl so intently, because you were destined to be with her through death. However, you're not dead, and you need to be reintegrated with the living—and she needs to be allowed to move on."

My head wouldn't stop spinning. I had just been told that I was supposed to be dead, and I was preventing my fiancée from crossing to the other side because I'd been holding on to her after she passed. Although I thought Hans might be right, it was still disturbing, and I felt more confused than ever.

He turned his back to me and faced the circle once again. "Cheryl, tell Scott: 'It was simply my time to go. I will see you again, although not for a while.'"

"It was simply my time to go. I will see you again, although not for a while," Cheryl said to my representative.

"I love you, but you need to let me go," Hans continued.

Cheryl repeated, "I love you, but you need to let me go."

I gasped as tears caught in my throat. I was finding it hard to breathe, and the lights fell to blackness as Cheryl's spirit finally moved away from me. My sadness flowed into relief, and for the first time since her death, I began to feel at peace with her passing.

"Because you're no longer on your natural path, you haven't been able to draw from the strength and support of your ancestors," Hans told my representative. "Your ancestors are willing to help you integrate a new path alongside theirs so you will no longer feel alone." He put his hands on the shoulders of my maternal grandfather and moved him to the left of my representative. He then guided my paternal grandfather to the right. My great-grandfather went to the left of my maternal grandfather, and the Cherokee nation to the opposite side.

Seeing my family surrounding me was extremely powerful. I felt loved and supported for the first time in years. With my ancestors flanking me like wings, I could imagine flying anywhere with their help.

Hans remained uncharacteristically quiet, and everyone within the circle looked nearly as worn-out as I felt. Faces were streaked with mascara, and wads of crumpled tissue littered the floor.

"Good," Hans finally said after a long silence. "Everyone in the field can return to their seats."

The representatives inside the circle wandered back to their chairs and gradually returned to being a group of people I didn't know. As they reclaimed their seats, pairs of concerned eyes turned to me as if to silently ask how I was doing.

Hans looked around as he addressed the entire group: "Everyone, close your eyes and once again breathe into your heart and exhale any energy from the field that remains inside you. It's important to release the energy from inside your body before you leave this room."

I followed his instructions and began to feel much lighter and more grounded than I had during the previous hour. It was finally over, and I felt an enormous sense of relief.

"What happened today in this constellation is a sacred bond between everyone who is here," Hans continued, "and it's important not to speak about it outside of this room. In fact, it will be most helpful for everyone"—and he looked right at me—"including you, Scott, if you try to forget what happened and allow the energy to work through you without letting your mind get in the way. I know it's difficult, but we moved a lot of energy today, and it will be many years from now before it all settles."

I wasn't sure what I was going to do with that information, but I did feel a lot better and was grateful. If he meant that I would gradually heal over the course of the following years, then I was all for it.

"Okay, we're done for now," said Hans abruptly. "Let's take a brief break and give Scott some time to settle in with his new support system."

Martika handed me a glass of water and asked if I was okay. Everything was still in a fog, but I felt much better. And definitely more interested in living than I had since Cheryl had passed. I knew she was finally gone, and for the first time in years I was ready to live again.

"Come on," said Martika. "Let me give you a ride home. I think you need to rest."

CHAPTER SEVEN

During the days following the soul retrieval and constellation, my senses were extremely heightened and my spirit was filled with a level of energy I hadn't felt in years. It was as if my soul finally had feelings of its own and was highly sensitive. Almost everything reminded me that my soul was there, and it was still tender to the touch. When I opened the window in my apartment, a happy person, a bird flying—even the wind—all seemed to poke my spirit and say, *You're finally alive.*

Since I was feeling so sensitive, I didn't leave my apartment for more than a week in order to recuperate. When I finally decided to get some fresh air, I had barely walked a block when I saw a girl in her early twenties with bright pink hair, a short skirt, and black-and-white striped socks skipping down the hill.

"Hello," I greeted her, feeling more friendly than I usually did.

"Hi there, I'm Om," she said in chipper voice while doing a little curtsy.

I wasn't sure I'd heard her right. "*M? Does that stand for something?*"

"No, Om. *O-M*. You know, like *Ommmm*." She pressed her thumbs to her middle fingers and cocked her head into an instant meditation pose. I counted eight earrings on one ear and only two on the other and worried that she'd tip over if she didn't straighten up quickly.

"I'm Scott," I finally said. "Nice to meet you, *Ommmm*."

She laughed. "I'm so happy! It's a beautiful day, and I'm going to kirtan, which always lifts my spirits."

I wasn't sure what she was talking about, but her energy was infectious. I could see it emanate from her body and enter mine, where my soul eagerly received her happiness. It was an incredible demonstration of the power of good intentions, and who better to be around than someone like Om, who was utterly filled with positive energy.

"Are you going to kirtan, also?" she asked.

"I don't know what that is."

"Oh, then you absolutely *must* come and meet my boyfriend, Garuda. Kirtan is the most beautiful experience in the world. You get a deep sense of inner peace and connectedness with the universe while you chant together with your fellow Earth spirits. Today it's in the park, and a beautiful flute player from Nepal will be there. I met him at a party last night, and he has the purest soul you'll ever meet. He can heal himself and others simply by playing his bamboo flute. It's so magical."

I didn't have any plans for the day, and although I wasn't familiar with what she was talking about, I could feel the excitement with her every breath. I also hadn't seen any live music in a while, and a concert in the park seemed like a great idea.

"Let's go," I said, and we made our way down the hill.

We walked on the sidewalk that bordered the park, and after passing two wooden bridges that spanned the creek, the Japanese garden came into view on the opposite side of the street. We crossed, and walked by the narrow garden, which was filled with bamboo, red-leaf miniature oak trees, and a trickling stream that meandered down the hill through the rock work.

We then came to a large sloping expanse of lawn flanked by three giant sequoias. The trees were enormously majestic and seemed delighted with the crowd of people quietly setting up blankets at the bases of their trunks. I hadn't seen so many people in the park before and was taken by the silence and peacefulness that accompanied their movements. Several were dressed in colorful, flowing fabrics; and a few were clad in nothing but white robes and turbans.

We found Om's boyfriend, Garuda, after a few minutes of wandering through the crowd, and he seemed genuinely happy to meet me. His head was shaved, and he was wearing a long white robe and a strand of large wrinkled seeds around his neck. Om introduced me in a soft voice, and after our whispered pleasantries, we all sat down to share a large white blanket. They both continued to talk in whispers, and although I couldn't hear everything they were saying, I could feel their energy welcoming me as a new friend. It was a sense of belonging I hadn't felt before with people I'd just met, and I enjoyed the unconditional feeling of community.

Garuda had reserved a spot in the center of the lawn, and we had a great view of the stage, which was covered in a large gilded rectangle of hand-woven fabric, with unusual-looking instruments situated among velvet pillows. The setting sun glistened on the instruments as the musicians emerged from the audience and took their positions.

The first sound came from a narrow cello-like instrument that sounded like a droning sitar floating through the air in a long, graceful ribbon. Garuda whispered the names of all the exotic instruments in my ear and explained that the first one was a tampura from India. After a few moments, an older-looking gentleman began to key the accordion-like instrument, called a harmonium. Then came the small silver tabla, a pair of drums that moved the audience to sway together in rhythm. And finally, a young Asian boy picked up an unassuming bamboo flute and began to make the most beautiful music I had ever heard. The notes flowed out of his hollowed instrument and floated over the audience right into my heart. I got chills with every long, drawn-out note that danced in and around a scale that was both foreign and familiar.

I had never heard music like that before, but it released something deep inside that had always been within me. His flute told a story of love and devotion, and tears of pure joy began to stream down my face. I had never cried for happiness before, but it felt so right that I decided it must be the best use of my tears.

The musicians let the flutist take the lead until an exotic-looking woman in a white robe and turban gracefully emerged from the audience and took her place in the center of the blanketed stage. She began to sing in a foreign language I didn't recognize, and intuitively the entire audience repeated the verse with a single grand and powerful voice. The first time it happened, there was a wave of energy that swirled among the audience members before dissipating into the sky above. She repeated the verse, and again the audience followed, even more powerful than before.

Initially I was reluctant to lend my voice to the collective, but as I listened closely and realized that many were not technically in tune, I discovered that the voices all blended together in a beautiful fabric not unlike nature itself. As I became more familiar with the chants, I started mouthing the lyrics first and then sang them aloud with everyone else.

"Govinda Jaya Jaya, Gopala Jaya Jaya"
Govinda Jaya Jaya, Gopala Jaya Jaya
"Radha Ramana Hari, Govinda Jaya Jaya"
Radha Ramana Hari, Govinda Jaya Jaya
"Govinda Jaya Jaya, Gopala Jaya Jaya"
Govinda Jaya Jaya, Gopala Jaya Jaya
"Radha Ramana Hari, Govinda Jaya Jaya"
Radha Ramana Hari, Govinda Jaya Jaya

The simple lyrics were repeated with little variation for nearly a half hour before the first song was complete. Once it was over, the audience fell into silence and let the stillness wash over them until the musicians began to weave their melodic yarn once again. By the middle of the second song, I stood and closed my eyes and sang from the bottom of my soul, and with each verse, I felt gradually more connected with everyone in the park. The lines between our bodies began to blur; and we became one moving, breathing mass of energy. I felt that I was literally transcending time and space with every verse, and after a number of songs, I couldn't feel my feet touching the grass anymore. My eyes could see that gravity was still employed, but my other senses weren't convinced.

The kirtan lasted nearly four hours, and when it came to a close, I was in a daze and could barely make my way home with Om and Garuda. After a few blocks of walking in silence, Om looked up to the sky while hugging herself and said, "I am so blissed out."

I followed her gaze, and although the stars were all shining, the moon was dark.

"It must be the new moon," I said.

"A time for rebirth," said Om as we turned onto my street.

"It certainly is." I smiled at both of them and glided up the walkway to my apartment. "Thank you."

"Namaste," they said in unison while pressing their palms together in a prayer position and gently bowing their heads.

That night I had the first of what was to become another recurring dream. I hadn't dreamed about Cheryl's accident since the constellation and was finally having restful nights for the first time in years. The new dream wasn't as frightening, but it was no less intense.

The dream took place in a small-town park I recognized as the one in Yreka where Cheryl and I used to spend a lot of time. It was a very special place for us, and we'd often walk through it at dusk during the height of summer when we first began dating. In the dream, I would begin by swinging on one particular swing on the far end of the swing set. It felt like I was waiting for someone or something, and after swinging for a short while, I would sense what seemed to be an energy portal that revealed itself immediately behind me. I never got close enough to touch it, but it began to grow until it was larger than the swing set itself.

At first I thought it was a symbolic dream that was allowing me to finally deal with Cheryl's death, but with every night, it became more and more powerful, and the feeling I had during it began to permeate my waking hours. After the dream had occurred every night for several days in a row, it began to consume me, and I could barely distinguish whether I was awake or asleep. I was obsessed with the portal above the swing set, and it felt as if Yreka held the key to another dimension of my spiritual awakening.

After what seemed to be nearly two weeks from when I started having the dream, it became clear to me that the portal would only be at the park on the following Friday. It didn't make sense logically, but it was as if time and space would intersect at a precise moment and reveal an "eclipse" to another dimension that only I seemed to know about. I was both drawn to and scared of what it represented, but I felt that I didn't have a choice. I *had* to find out what it was. I knew that my spiritual journey had just begun, but somehow I felt that the portal would transport me to another place spiritually and accelerate my journey.

I still hadn't seen Robert since my soul retrieval, and it seemed like a good idea to check in with him while I was considering following my dreams to Yreka. The anger I felt toward him for abandoning me had dissipated, and I'd begun to come to terms with the fact that he was a free spirit who would float in and out of my life whenever the time was right. And on this day I sensed that the time was indeed right to see him again, and I was pretty sure I knew exactly where he would be.

I made my way to the Co-op and saw him sitting cross-legged with his back against his favorite tree, Puppy Don at his feet and a smaller-than-normal cardboard sign resting on his lap:

Listen to your heart.

"Hi, Robert!"

"Wow, you look different," Robert said while scanning me up and down. "How have your dreams been?"

"Funny you ask, that's why I'm here." His intuitive ability *was* remarkable.

"I figured as much. What do your dreams say?"

"They've been telling me to go to Yreka and swing on a swing set." I tried to make light of it.

"And what's *at* the swing set?"

"It seems like a portal to another dimension." I had never said it out loud before, and it sounded kind of corny. "Is that possible?"

"Of course it's possible."

"Why would I be dreaming that?"

"When people dream, a portion of their soul is free to leave the body and mingle with the collective unconscious. Sometimes it's just for fun, like flying dreams. Other times it's to retrieve ancient wisdom or power. Now that you have the guidance of your ancestors, they are helping you become stronger."

"So do you think I should go?"

"What do *you* think?"

"I think so."

"Did the dream give you a time?"

"Yes—this Friday."

"Hmm, it sounds like the real deal. It's probably some sort of vision quest for you."

"What's a vision quest?"

"It's a Native American coming-of-age journey where adolescents are sent into the wilderness to overcome obstacles and glimpse a view of their future. And it sounds like Yreka might be your 'wilderness.' Does it scare you?"

"A little bit."

"Good, it should. If you choose to do it, you need to go with an open heart and mind and not have any preconceived thoughts about what you'll discover. Vision quests can be one of the most powerful experiences of a spiritual journey, and there's no point in going unless you are completely present."

"Okay."

"It seems like your heart is now much more open than it has been. When we first met, you were closed up like a clamshell, and nothing could get in. Do you understand?"

I did feel a lot more open than before, and I never wanted to be closed off from the world again. "I think so," I finally said aloud.

"I think you should go," he said after a long pause. "How are you going to get there? Isn't your car dead?"

I had been so caught up in the dream that I'd forgotten about the practical. "Oh yeah. A car."

"I think Martika has an extra one she lets people from the constellation group use on occasion. Why don't you see if you can borrow it."

"That's a good idea."

"Good luck, Scott. I hope you find what you're looking for. You are at a very special place in your journey."

"Thank you, Robert. I'll let you know what I find."

"I'm counting on it."

CHAPTER EIGHT

left Ashland early Friday morning and excitedly scaled the Siskiyous in Martika's spare car, which thankfully handled the ascent with much more grace than my old Volvo had. As I neared the California border, the optimistic hues of the Oregonian evergreens were replaced with the muted tones of death and dying, as if Mother Nature drew an imaginary line to divide the greens from golds.

When I crossed the border, it felt as if my spirit, *my life force,* began to seep out the back of my neck, as if it were attached to a string and secured to the Oregon side. The longer I continued to drive away from that imaginary line, the more I felt empty inside, until nearly all the sharpness had dulled from every one of my senses. Everything smelled and tasted like dust. Even sipping from the bottle of springwater I'd brought for the drive tasted dusty. The feeling in my fingertips became numb, and all of a sudden it felt like I was wearing knitted gloves. The sound of the car's wheels on the pavement was far in the distance, as if my hearing were muffled by imaginary cotton balls. And nearly all the brightest hues outside had faded from my vision, and everything I could see was tinted with warm sepia tones, as though I were looking at an old-fashioned photograph.

Luckily my muscle memory seemed to take over, and I began driving on autopilot, without my brain and hands needing to communicate any longer. At first I started to panic, but I began to breathe deeply and even caught myself closing my eyes. I was lucid enough to realize that even driving on autopilot required my eyelids to stay open, which took a remarkable amount of will to maintain. Once, after catching myself dozing off, I shook myself awake, and the first thing I saw when I opened my eyes was the majestic Mount Shasta. It appeared to glow with a bright white halo, which contrasted with the muted tones surrounding it. I'd always felt a connection with Mount Shasta when

I was growing up, and although I had no plans to reach the summit that day, I made a mental note to revisit the mountain as soon as I could.

The closer I got to Yreka, the more I began to get used to my deadened sensory state. And other than one last scare when I headed straight for the guardrail on the steep mountain pass, I was much more coherent during the remaining trip.

When I arrived in Yreka, I was surprised by how empty it seemed. It had always been a small town, but now it appeared nearly deserted. There were no cars on the streets, no birds in the sky, and no pedestrians on the sidewalks. Perhaps my dulled senses were playing tricks on me, but it felt like even the breeze had decided to abandon the old mining town and leave the stillness of the air to imprison all that remained.

After parking in a mini-mart lot, I retraced my path back to the cement island that had greeted me immediately after I exited the freeway. I thought that I recognized some people I knew out of the corner of my eye when I drove past the bronze sculpture of a miner and mule underneath the blue and white tiled YREKA sign. I knew that it was impossible, since I was sure that everyone from my past had left the area many years before, yet I permitted a twinge of excitement to lead me back to the sculpture to find out if what I'd seen had been real or imagined.

As I neared the backside of the sculpture, I was both excited and a bit nervous to discover that the people I'd seen were still there. Standing next to the miner was a young brown-haired boy with a shaggy bowl haircut and his balding father, who had a bushy sandy-blond beard. The closer I got, the more I could hear their conversation, and it chilled me when I recognized their voices.

"Many people came to Siskiyou County during the gold rush to claim their fortunes," the father explained. *"But few succeeded, and most left penniless."*

"Dad, are we going to find gold here?"

"Probably not. But if we work hard enough, we can be the ones to fix the miners' equipment when it breaks."

I remembered the conversation word for word when my family first arrived in Yreka after moving there from Southern California. Yreka was about twenty miles from the town of Greenview, where we eventually settled, but it was that bronze sculpture that had represented the optimism we'd all felt when we first arrived. The possibilities had seemed limitless, and we were all excited to have enough land where we could raise animals and grow our own food. My well-intentioned father had grown up in the heartland of Iowa, and although my mother was a Southern California girl through and through, he convinced her that the country was a much better place to raise children; and at the beginning, I too bought into this idea.

When I circled to the front of the sculpture, the man and child were no longer there, and I immediately fell to my knees and began to weep. I had fallen out of touch with my family, and although we maintained contact through occasional phone calls on birthdays and holidays, my tears finally seemed to express the lack of connection I felt. The bronze statue was exactly the same, but I was no longer the wide-eyed little boy excited about a new adventure, and my father was no longer the idealistic mechanic eager to fix mining equipment. The years had eroded our optimism to reveal pessimism—his financially and mine socially. When we finally felt defeated by Siskiyou County, we both retreated to our respective birthplaces: my father took my mother and sister to Iowa to be near his family, and I left Cheryl's grave on my way to Southern California, where I thought I'd be able to invent a new family that would be more like me.

After about ten minutes at the foot of the bronze sculpture, I wiped the tears from my eyes, dusted myself off, and began to walk toward Miner Street. I'd come to Yreka to visit the park, but I wasn't sure I was ready quite yet. I was feeling both fragile and nostalgic and decided to reminisce by visiting a few shops in the town center before going to the park.

On Miner Street, the buildings still had the same old-fashioned façades from the late 1800s; however, years of neglect made it seem more like a decaying ghost town than a vibrant celebration of happier times. A few of the same shops still existed, and an old memory popped into my consciousness with nearly every step. The memories were flooding in when I found myself at the door of the sporting-goods store at the top of the street.

Looking up, I recognized the carved wooden sign in the shape of a green fish hanging above the entrance. I carefully opened the glass door and recognized all the sights and smells from my youth and was instantly transported to my thirteenth birthday. My father had brought me to this very shop on that day, and I remembered the distinct smell of gunpowder mixed with the stench of rotting cheese and salmon eggs. The shelves were still packed with guns, fishing poles, ammunition, and all the paraphernalia needed to quickly and violently destroy any of our fellow nature friends.

As the door shut behind me, I could see three generations of old-timers sitting on green vinyl-covered bar stools and sipping steaming black coffee while talking to the store owner. They were all wearing matching pearl-buttoned cowboy shirts and grease-stained baseball caps with tractor company logos stitched on the fronts. Their dust-worn, gravelly voices intertwined with the uncomfortable memory of my thirteenth birthday.

"I'm going to get my grandson this ought-six for Christmas."

"Today I'm going to show you the gun that will be yours if you keep your grades up."

"That's quite a gun for a thirteen-year-old. It'll knock him on his keister."

The store filled with laughter that nearly masked a coughing fit from the eldest.

"This is the same gun my father gave me when I was your age, and if you weren't so far behind in school, it would already be yours. A gun like this will make you a man."

"Yeah, but he's a darn-near sharpshooter with his .22. Can shoot beer cans from 300 yards without a scope."

"I wish I had his peepers. I would've got that six-pointer a couple years back."

"You and that six-pointer. I don't think I believe you even saw it anymore."

The other two roared with laughter, and this time the coughing fit went on for a solid thirty seconds.

"It would be a shame if your lackadaisical attitude in school prevented you from becoming a man. Do you hear me?"

I'm not sure where my father got the idea that I bought into his theory that you needed to kill innocent animals to become a man, but I had always been secretly proud that I helped save wildlife by letting my grades slip. To be honest, I'd been bored by the curriculum in the new school, which was almost two years behind what I had been learning before I moved. And by the time my new school had caught up, I felt I was so superior to everyone there, including most of the teachers, that I never bothered to do any homework—until I finally dropped out three years later.

Mounted high on the wall of the shop were two deer heads frozen in time while locking their blood-covered horns. Both their long tongues were hanging out, and all four eyes had rolled to the backs of their heads in agony, as they clearly hadn't passed on peaceful terms. The sight of the deer heads instantly transported me to the first time my father and I had gone hunting, a few months after my thirteenth birthday. Since my report card hadn't arrived yet, he'd lent me one of his guns, which was way too big for me.

"We'll tell your mother you got this one yourself. I'm proud of you, son."

In truth I had nicked the deer's back right leg with my shaky aim, and my father had finished it off with the second fatal shot before it had a chance to limp off into the wild. I was speechless as I stood over the deer and wondered how I could have been involved in taking such a beautiful life away from its family.

My father thrust a large hunting knife into my small hands; and with his hand squeezing tightly around my fingers, he steadied the blade at the base of the deer's long, smooth neck.

"Come on, son, you have to move quickly. If you don't bleed him in the first couple minutes, you'll ruin the meat."

I tried to pull the knife away from the deer with all my strength, but my father squeezed my fingers until it felt like he was going to crush them. He then pushed the knife deliberately into the innocent's flesh, and bright red liquid began to foam and gush. . . .

My stomach immediately grew queasy, and I almost passed out in the sporting-goods store. I was instantly light-headed and could feel my face turn pale. I stumbled to the door and pushed it open while gasping for air.

"I believe he just saw Bambi and his little brother." I heard the shopkeeper laugh as the door shut behind me with a muted thump.

Once outside, I tripped on the curb and scraped my right knee through my faded blue jeans. I decided to stay seated on the curb until I could catch my breath. Returning to Yreka was bringing up some deep-seated memories I hadn't even known I still had, and I was getting nervous about returning to the park because I wasn't sure if I could handle what was next. I considered getting in the car and driving back to Ashland without even going near it, but I knew that if I didn't go then, I never would. And if there was something to my feeling that the portal was only accessible on that day, I would forever regret not finding out what it was for.

After about ten minutes—when I had recovered from my experience at the sporting-goods store enough to continue on—I picked myself up and started toward the park at the top of the hill. I was only a couple of blocks away, and my stomach fluttered when I saw the blackened granite archway that marked the entrance. I had spent many hours in this park with Cheryl, but even during all those years I had never really looked at the hand-carved lettering that adorned the imposing archway. Beneath the name of the park was the word SISKIYOU inscribed in large, ghostlike letters that seemed to dance in place. The name of the county where

Yreka resided seemed an odd choice for prominent billing, but most eerie were the letters themselves, which appeared to mirror my every gesture.

The park itself was divided in three sections. The one closest to the archway was a walking area where several large, stately trees had been planted amid occasional benches so visitors could lounge under the ample shade. On the opposite end was a baseball diamond that was the perfect size for Little League games, and to the left was the playground that contained the swing set I'd seen in my dreams.

I was pulled toward the swings with a gravity I couldn't control, and within seconds I was standing near the one that had been adjacent to the portal from my dream. However, the swing set was already occupied by two young redheaded girls being pushed by a middle-aged man with short red hair and a green and purple pin-striped buttoned shirt. The girls were both wearing yellow flowered sundresses, and the youngest had two matching flesh-colored bandages on her knees.

I could tell that I made the father nervous, and assumed that not many grown men hung around swing sets in Yreka by themselves. I tried sitting in the swing next to where the girls were playing and discovered that it was clearly designed for children less than half my size. I barely fit into the small seat, and my knees nearly scraped the sand as the chains loudly squeaked under the stress of my weight. And as soon as I started swinging, the father began to whisper to his children about leaving, while he squinted his green eyes at me with apparent disapproval. I hadn't intended to make anyone uncomfortable, so I exited the child swing and tried to casually browse the park-bench dedications while waiting for the family to finish.

In my boredom I approached them again and attempted to put them at ease. "Beautiful day," I said to the father.

"Uh-huh." His incredulity was intense.

"I'm waiting for my niece," I said, hoping my white lie would help. "She loves that swing."

"Oh, I see." The man smiled, and I could tell that he was much more relaxed than he had been since I'd arrived. "We're almost done. It's the best swing in the park, so I can see why you're waiting for it."

"Yeah, it's the only one she likes. She made me come down here and get dibs on it." I laughed as my white lie became more intricate with every syllable.

"We should probably get going. Come on, girls, we really have to go now." The three of them waved goodbye as they left the park and walked up Miner Street toward the houses in the hills.

As soon as the family left, I immediately went to the swing from my dream. It felt a lot like the first one—very short and squeaky, and not very satisfying for someone of my size. But more significant, there was definitely not a portal, and like the rest of Yreka, the park seemed completely devoid of any spiritual energy.

Confused and frustrated, I began to walk around the perimeter of the park to see if I could find the portal I had dreamed about. I kept retracing my steps, and I put the palms of my hands on every tree near the swing set to see if I could feel anything. There was a second swing set perpendicular to the one I'd seen in my dreams, and in my desperation, I went over to it and started swinging. These were "big person" swings with large rubber rectangles for seats and stainless-steel chains that were attached nearly twenty feet above the ground.

The bigger swings were much more suited to my size, and although I didn't feel anything supernatural, I did enjoy swinging on them for a few minutes. I even considered being brave enough to jump off when the swing was at its highest point in order to see how far I could fly before hitting the ground, but I wisely decided to wait until it had settled before getting off.

Discouraged, I sat on the grass and stared at the swings, wondering if I had misinterpreted my dream. Perhaps my vision quest was already over and had simply been about coming to terms with my childhood. Or maybe it was supposed to be on a different day, and either I was too early or my opportunity had passed.

Just as I was about to give up, I noticed a swing that was wrapped around a post, tied up and out of commission. I carefully unwound it from the post, and it fell into place. As it settled, I was perplexed to notice that it didn't seem to have a shadow. I looked at the other swings and *they* all did, but the one in front of me didn't appear to. I knew that it was physically impossible for one swing not to cast a shadow, so I convinced myself that it was an optical illusion of some sort and tried my best to ignore it.

I cautiously lowered myself into the swing and pushed off with my legs. I almost immediately felt a sharp stabbing pain in my abdomen. I swung my legs back and forth, and with every swing, the pain in my stomach became more and more intense. I began to sweat profusely, and within seconds I shot out of the swing and hit the sand hard. The impact knocked the breath out of my lungs, and when I looked back toward the swing, I was shocked to see that it was already motionless, as if I'd never been on it.

Terrified, I stood up and tried to run to the opposite end of the park, but my legs wouldn't move. The more I tried, the more my muscles froze, and I found myself falling backward in slow motion until the ground slapped my back with a force that ensured my breath wouldn't soon return.

Staring up at the sky, I could see the clouds turning from an innocuous white to a menacing dark gray as they began to swirl above the park. The clouds circled slowly at first, then quickly picked up momentum until there was a visible funnel coming toward the park. I still couldn't breathe or move my body, and my fear was replaced with genuine panic as the twister's funnel descended. Within seconds the entire sky darkened, and I could feel the twister connect with my abdomen.

The pain was excruciating—it felt like the funnel was sucking my organs out of my body and flinging them into the sky above. I tried to scream with all of my might, but only silence came out of my mouth while I gasped for air with a violently painful dry heave. And at that very moment, the park filled with the most petrifying sound I'd ever heard. It was the noise of all the anger that fueled every roar that had ever existed, the sound of the fear that powered every scream since the beginning of time, and the wailing of every baby that had ever been born. The piercing sound was absolutely deafening, and as the light dimmed to near black, I felt as if I'd begun to float above the ground.

Through the darkness I could barely make out the grotesque mouths that were responsible for all the screams I was hearing. Their twisted faces swirled within the cyclone and began to impale me, one after another, plunging deep inside my abdomen. With every soul that entered me, the pain became more and more intolerable, until I closed my eyes and clenched my teeth as tightly as I could.

Within seconds the roar was replaced by the sound of a single screaming baby, and when I opened my eyes, I could see that I was floating face-down above a crib, and the baby was screaming at *me.* The veins in its temples were nearly popping

out of its head, and I could tell that I was terrifying the infant with my very presence. To the right
of the crib I saw a television set that was showing
black-and-white static, and I immediately recognized that the child was me as an infant.

When I was just a few months old, my parents
would leave the television on in my room, and the
screen would turn to static after the stations went
off the air. Once this happened, nearly every night
a large dark figure would hover above my crib and
gesture for me to join it. Instinctively I knew that
whatever it was didn't have the purest of intentions; and I would close my eyes and let out a long,
silent scream until it left. I'd always wished that
someone could hear my cries for help, but whenever the entity appeared, my vocal cords became
paralyzed, and I would be forced to face it alone.
In retrospect I'm convinced that it was coming for
my young soul. I don't know how I protected myself at such an early age, but thankfully it quit appearing by the time I could speak.

But now it was back, and it was once again
coming for me, this time with much less restraint
than it had before.

By then my abdomen was filled with literally
hundreds of souls, all connecting me to the same

dark entity I had feared as an infant, and they attached me strand by strand to a grotesquely writhing braided cord that disappeared far into the darkness.

I struggled to regain my strength, and when I had nearly resigned myself to defeat, a familiar scene revealed itself. I was once again back at Cheryl's accident, but this time the drunk driver got out of the car and started to approach me, laughing. He continued his chilling cackle as he walked past Cheryl, past my mother, past the police officer, and headed directly toward me. In the hundreds of times I'd experienced the dream before, I had only been an observer. But this was no dream, and the drunk driver definitely saw me there. I had never seen his face before, but as he came closer, I recognized him—and my blood ran cold. I completely lost all consciousness when I saw his face.

It was *me*.

CHAPTER NINE

I didn't remember driving back to Ashland, but I must have, because the next thing I recalled was waking up on the floor of my apartment. I was still fully clothed with my shoes on, and evidently I'd tried to make a bed on the living-room floor out of sofa cushions and blankets. I had no idea why I hadn't made it to the bedroom, but I was probably in quite a state, since two of the lamps were knocked over and the coffee table was propped up against the wall on its side.

My abdomen was still in severe pain, and I felt completely drained and had a throbbing headache. I slowly began to remember what happened in Yreka, and when the terrifying memories returned,

I knew that I needed some serious help. I considered going to the hospital, but I wasn't sure how to explain to the doctors what had happened. In fact, I wasn't sure how to explain to *myself* what had happened. I finally decided that Robert was my best bet, and I hoped I could find him at the Co-op, because I knew I didn't have the energy to make it to his tipi.

As I staggered outside, I noticed Martika's car parked at an angle on the sidewalk, with the backside jutting into the street. Underneath the bumper were two trash cans that had emptied their contents all over the sidewalk. I knew the car should be moved and the garbage picked up, but I barely had enough energy to walk. And with my head swimming like it was, I knew I wasn't in any state to drive. So I stumbled down the hill to the Co-op, and as soon as I approached, Robert ran up to me.

"What happened to you?" he asked with genuine concern that I'd never heard from him before.

"The swing set . . ." I said in a shaky voice. "My stomach hurts."

"I bet it hurts—you have a huge black cloud around your torso. We should go to your apartment now; you're in need of some serious healing."

He slung Puppy Don over his shoulder like a bag of rice and with his hand on the small of my back, guided me up the hill. As we neared my apartment, he saw Martika's car parked on the sidewalk and shook his head compassionately.

"I should have given you some protection," he said as I unlocked my door. "I didn't think they would be after you so quickly."

"*Who* is after me?"

"We'll talk about that later. Why don't you grab a pillow and some blankets and join me in the backyard. This will be much easier in nature."

I found some extra bedding and met Robert outside. He had just finished moving the cedar picnic table under the large madrone tree.

"Lie down on the table, faceup, and close your eyes," he said as he took the bedding and folded it to create a makeshift bed on top of the picnic table. "We need to get to work."

Robert put one hand on my abdomen and the other on my forehead and began to breathe deeply. He moved his hands to different parts of my body and inhaled through his nose and exhaled loudly out of his mouth. Then he began mumbling in a barely discernible voice.

"Uh-huh. Yes, I know. Yes. Oh, I see. You'll be okay. You can be open without being vulnerable. Uh-huh. Okay. There. I understand."

He then put his thumb and forefinger on either side of my arm and firmly squeezed toward my hand while abruptly pulling on my fingers as if he was extracting tar out of each one.

I opened my eyes and saw seven dragonflies flying in triangles over my head. I could almost touch them with my nose as they appeared to canvass the space immediately above me. There was also a single bright blue dragonfly that was hovering about a foot above the triangle, apparently supervising the procession.

"Fairy spirits," I said feebly.

"Yes, you're lucky. They're helping a lot today."

As soon as Robert had finished with all ten fingers, he moved to my legs and did the same with my toes. As he did so, a warm sensation flowed through my limbs, and I could feel the color return to my face. Once he finished, the pain in my stomach began to throb with even more intensity.

"My stomach," I said.

"Shhh . . . I know . . . I'm going to work on your stomach next."

He slowly moved his hands up the sides of my torso and rested both of them on my lower abdomen. He started to breathe even more deeply than before. As he exhaled, he started coughing uncontrollably but kept his hands on me. After his third breathing and coughing fit, there was a huge rush of energy that filled my entire torso, starting with my abdomen and flooding into my heart and up my spine. I felt whole again, as if I'd just woken from the dead. I opened my eyes and could see Robert bent over with tears streaming down his face.

"I'm so sorry," he said, making no effort to hide his tears.

"What happened?"

"You were bitten."

"Bitten?" I was confused. "By what?"

He continued as if he hadn't heard the question: ". . . and after you were bitten, they attached an energy cord to your abdomen. That's why you were drained. They were literally sucking the energy right out of you."

"Who did this to me?" I was starting to get angry. "And why would they do that?"

"Because you are getting too powerful."

"Who did this to me?" I was getting very annoyed that he wouldn't answer me. "Robert, tell me who did this to me!"

"There are two modes of thought about this type of thing. The most popular view is that *it* is never acknowledged under any circumstances, and most spiritual people will even go as far as denying *it* exists."

"*What* exists? Robert, stop talking in circles and tell me what happened to me!"

"Evil," he said as he looked to the ground. "Evil," he repeated after a long pause. "Many healers believe that if you acknowledge evil, then you give it more power. But sometimes, not knowing it exists is more dangerous than ignoring it. It's a dilemma I've faced for many years, and although many elders say to avoid giving it any power at all costs, in your case you need to know so you can protect yourself."

My head was spinning, "What does evil have to do with *me?*"

"It wants to stop you, and unfortunately, I don't think this will be the last time it will try."

"Stop me from what?"

"From bringing more light into the world. You are destined to be a great healer, and you've attracted the attention of evil. Right now you don't have all of your tools, so at this point in time you're the most vulnerable. If it can stop you now, then you will never be a threat."

"But why did it happen in Yreka? In the park?"

"Actually, Yreka contains *many* negative energy portals. It's between Mount Ashland and Mount Shasta, which are two powerful positive energy vortexes. In fact, Shasta is one of the most powerful vortexes in all of North America."

"But why would there be so much negative energy in between two positive places?"

"Because the dark follows the light. It's like a moth to a flame: it can't get too close or it will disappear, but it can't keep itself from being attracted. All spiritual leaders have a constant struggle with negative forces, and when someone is transitioning to an enlightened soul, that's when they are most vulnerable."

"Why didn't you warn me?"

"I didn't think . . ." His words trailed off. ". . . Yes, I should have warned you, and I'm sorry."

"But why did it happen? Why was it so important for me to go to Yreka?"

"You were drawn there because your soul is starting to communicate on multiple levels, and you are quickly opening up to other dimensions."

"What does that mean?" I was more confused than ever.

"It means you are now opening up to the spirit world; and you can see, hear, and—in this case—*feel* energy on a soul level, in addition to your physical reality. Most people's senses have been trained to focus on only what's happening in the physical world, but you're quickly overcoming those arbitrary limitations."

"So does that mean I went to Yreka because I was finally able to hear the spirit world calling?"

"Yes, that's part of it. But now you need to learn to protect yourself until you can discern light from dark energy."

"And how do I do that?"

"You'll need to find a teacher who can train you about these things, but in the meantime you should be careful, and be wary of being called to the spirit world while you're still vulnerable."

"Can't *you* teach me?"

"No," he chuckled. "I'm in the physical world for the time being. You need to find a teacher you can trust who's already in the spirit world."

"And how will I know who I can trust?"

"Listen to your heart—you will know. And if you're not sure, then the answer is probably no. We can talk about this more later, but I'm going to the store to get some supplies to finish today's healing—I'll be right back."

After he left, I went inside my apartment. I opened the refrigerator to pour myself a glass of water and found the car keys sitting inside on the butter tray. Shaking my head and letting out a long sigh, I decided to move the car to a more respectable parking place and return the garbage to the crushed bins.

While I was picking up the trash, I reflected on what Robert had said. I didn't want to go back to Yreka, that was for sure. And I definitely didn't want to risk finding myself in such a terrifying situation again. But on some level I felt that there was something in the spirit world that was part of my destiny. Although I knew I needed to recover from what had happened in Yreka, I felt that whatever it was had permanently changed me and there was no going back.

About twenty minutes later, Robert let himself inside my apartment carrying a small paper bag. "I'm going to make you a healing bath," he said.

I followed him as he went into my bathroom and turned on the tap. "I cut a rather large energy cord that was attached to you, and you now have a big hole in your abdomen where it was. This bath of sea salt and cider vinegar will help you heal."

The entire apartment filled with the pungent smell of vinegar, and after a few minutes, he turned off the tap and gestured for me to get in the tub.

"I want you to soak for twenty minutes and then crawl in your bed and rest for the remainder of the day. I'll stop by and check on you tomorrow, but I think you're going to be okay."

He let himself out of my apartment, and I submerged myself in the pungent bath. I soaked for his prescribed twenty minutes and began to feel much better. Worn-out but better. I was definitely upset with Robert for not warning me about what might be after me, but I also felt blessed that I had someone guiding me through these experiences.

I wasn't sure what was in store for me, but I felt that I was on the edge of something very significant. It was as if my life was becoming bigger than myself, and I was about to bear responsibilities that were of great consequence. However, I was worried: if a simple swing set could do what it did to me, how would I have the strength to be of service to anyone else? I tried to garner the trust that the universe wasn't going to give me anything I couldn't handle, and resolved to stay as grounded as possible during what was turning out to be an unforgettable journey.

CHAPTER TEN

The next morning the telephone woke me up and Martika was on the other end.

"Hi, Scott. How are you feeling?"

"Much better, thank you. Did Robert tell you what happened in Yreka?"

"Yes, he did. I'm sorry you had to go through that. But it's sort of a rite of passage, as they say."

"Yeah, I guess so."

"It just means you're on the right path."

"That's what Robert says."

"He's a great teacher. I've known him for many lifetimes."

"Do you believe in evil?" I was still coming to terms with what had happened in Yreka.

"Oh, I don't know about that. I know Robert has very strong opinions about such things, but my experience has shown me that negative energy can usually be reversed with healing."

"So being mean is just a sickness?"

"I guess you could say that," she laughed. "I'm not saying there isn't dark energy, but I've seen some pretty horrific souls heal and become harmless once their core issues have been dealt with."

I hadn't told Robert about the face I'd seen on the drunk driver, but I felt I really needed to share what had happened. I told Martika all I could remember and asked her what she thought.

"When you saw your face on the drunk driver, what did you feel?" she asked after a long silence.

"I don't know—I passed out."

"What do you feel about it now?"

"Anger. I don't know. Guilt?"

"Guilt is a step in the right direction. That means you're starting to be able to identify with him on some level. Many people try to come to terms with their own shadow, but the ultimate goal is to come to terms with *humanity's* shadow. That's where the big healing is done."

"What do you mean by 'shadow'?" I felt like I should probably already know what Martika was talking about, but she made me feel comfortable about asking questions that Robert would find annoying.

"Within everyone is both our dark side and our light side. We can't be fully integrated and balanced without accepting that both are important aspects of being human. People who ignore or try to hide their dark side from themselves or others become quite depressed, or in some cases, much worse. When their darkness finally bubbles up to the surface after it can no longer be contained, some very extreme things can happen."

"Like when people yell at you for no reason?"

"Yes, that—and unfortunately, much, much worse."

I let my mind reflect on the nightly news, and I wondered how many tragedies could be averted if people weren't trying to subvert their shadows.

"And the gift you've been given," Martika continued, "is to realize that humanity has a collective light side and a collective shadow side that we are all a part of. We are all connected, and you were shown a literal example of this. Yes, your love of Cheryl is a given. But you are also the drunk driver who killed her. And so am I. We are all love, and we are all hate. We are one, with all of our colors."

"That's a bit hard to take." I was attempting to be as diplomatic as possible while trying to distinguish between my feelings of anger and confusion. There was no way I could imagine taking responsibility for being the drunk driver that took Cheryl away from me.

"Yes, it *is* hard to take, Scott. I'm sorry you had to learn this with such a painful lesson. Truly, my heart goes out to you."

"So you're saying that everyone is inherently good?" I asked with a sense of indignation that was difficult to hide. "That seems at odds with Robert's view."

"That's true," she laughed, "we don't agree on everything. And Robert does have more experience than I do with these types of things, so do follow his advice and be wary. But also remember to look for the good in everyone, no matter how hard it is to find. Because when you can help someone heal, you are helping *everyone* heal."

"We are all connected."

"Yes, we are." She paused. "I'm sorry to change the subject, but a friend of mine needs to use the car tomorrow . . ."

"Oh, I'm so sorry. I'll bring it right over."

"I don't need it until tonight. And if you're up for it, I'm having a small gathering—you could bring the car over tonight and meet some new people."

"That sounds fantastic . . . I'll be there."

Martika gave me the details, and I began to get ready to reenter the world for the first time since my Yrekan vision quest.

I arrived ten minutes early to Martika's stately country house after putting some gas into her car, and was surprised to find that her party was already in full swing. She answered the door wearing a hand-painted blue and white silk dress and a large white flower in her hair.

"You look good," Martika said as she gave me a big hug. "Are you fully recovered?"

"I think so—thanks for asking." Martika always seemed to have the right thing to say.

The inside of the house was decorated with an unusual blend of contemporary and country-farmhouse sensibilities. The floors looked like the original hardwood planks that had the charm and history of many years of living. And the original

wood finishings were accented with dramatic contemporary and Asian-inspired artwork that filled
the walls. In the entryway, an imposing cream-
colored Buddha greeted the guests. There was
something mysterious about the large collage, and
as I neared it to get a better look, I was shocked by
what I saw.

"Is this made of cigarettes?"

"Yes," Martika said. "A local artist unrolls used
cigarettes he gathers from bars around town and
collages them to make the most amazing pieces."

"Do you smoke?" I was finding it difficult to
resolve the disparity between Martika's image and
a wall full of used cigarettes. As I looked closer, I
recoiled in disgust when I realized that Buddha's
crimson mouth was composed of lipstick-stained
papers.

"Oh, heavens no. But this piece repulses me
so much that I just had to have it. And I promised
myself I would hang it in a prominent place until
I am able to accept it completely and fully. I guess
I'm sort of addicted to healing. I'm immediately
drawn to anything that makes me uncomfortable
because I know there's something underneath that
I need to work on."

Martika gestured for me to follow her, and as we moved through the hallway into her beautiful home, she had one last thing to say on the subject: "My father used to smoke."

When we entered the kitchen, there were several people I recognized from the constellation group and a few more who didn't look familiar. They were of all ages, but once again, mostly female. It seemed like the large country-style kitchen was the heart of the party, and many guests were gathered near the bright blue and red pots that were bubbling on the restaurant-style stainless-steel stove.

"There are a bunch of great people here for you to meet," Martika said. "Can I get you some water or tea?"

"Tea would be great."

"I hope you like rooibos," she said as she handed me a cup of steaming red liquid.

"This tastes amazing." I loved the tart, nutty flavor that was unlike any other tea I'd had before. "Where can you get it?"

"It's from Africa, but you can get it at the Co-op, of course."

"Of course." I smiled.

"Oh, Scott, I want you to meet Lisa from the group. She was in the constellation with you, and I think you have a lot in common." Martika introduced me to a short perky brunette with curly hair and bright red lipstick. After making sure we were properly acquainted, Martika brought the teapot into the other room and left the two of us to talk in the kitchen.

"Wow, your constellation was so intense," said Lisa, speaking much faster than I was used to listening. "I know we're not supposed to talk about it, but I've never seen anything like that before."

"Have you seen a lot of them?" I finally remembered her sitting next to the "mustache" at the constellation.

"I'm in the yearlong intensive, so I go to a three-day weekend every month and sometimes a few other times, like the one you were in."

"That's a lot. I don't know if I could handle doing that every month, let alone three days in a row."

"You get used to it, but I think your session was a bit more intense than most."

That made me feel a bit better. I couldn't imagine it getting more intense than that!

"I was shocked when Hans said you were sup-posed to be dead," Lisa continued. "I totally got truth bumps when he said that."

"'Truth bumps'?"

"You know, goose pimples, goose flesh, chills—whatever you call it. When the hair stands up on the back of your neck."

"Oh."

"Do you know why truth bumps happen?"

"Nope."

"They happen when the connection to your spirit is stronger than the connection to your body. And that's why I knew that what Hans said was true. How did you feel when he said you were supposed to be dead?"

"At first I was angry, but then I felt relieved." I was surprised at myself for being so open with someone I barely knew, but being in Martika's house made me feel safe. "I'm relieved because now I know I wasn't imagining it. I'd always felt I was supposed to be dead, but it didn't make any sense until he explained it."

"Wow, that's so intense."

Martika reappeared, clinking her glass with the handle of a fork. "Everyone, please move into the dining room. Dinner is ready!"

We proceeded into the dining room, which had two large dining tables butted up against each other. On the long wall hanging above the tables was a horizontal cigarette-paper collage of the Last Supper that seemed to ominously supervise all that would be consumed in the room. There were nearly twenty place settings, and everyone took their positions behind their chairs and intuitively held hands with one another. I wasn't used to holding hands with people I didn't know, but there was a genuine innocence about it that seemed to make the evening more charming.

I was positioned between two gray-topped ladies I hadn't met before. One was wearing a red velvet dress and had shoulder-length hair; the other was in green velvet, with her curly locks cropped close. The longer-haired lady loosely held my left hand, her cold, clammy palm barely pressing against mine; and the other gripped my fingers tightly, smiling a wide, toothy grin. She made me feel uncomfortable with her presumed intimacy, but I tried to be friendly and smiled back as warmly as I could.

"Thank you all for coming," said Martika, raising her glass. "You are all very dear to me, and I'm happy to be able to bring you together on this special night. Since many of you haven't met before, please take a moment and introduce yourselves before we eat."

Everyone took their turn introducing themselves, and mostly they all sounded the same. "Hi, I'm so-and-so, and I'm in the X-year intensive," or "I'm who's-her-face, and I'm going to go to my first constellation next week." However, one person stood out from the crowd during the introductions—a well-dressed young lady with long curly blonde hair who looked like she could be Martika's younger sister. She was wearing a simple white blouse and a flowing powder blue cotton skirt that scalloped to the floor in the shape of a three-layer cake.

"Hi, I'm Madisyn with a *y*—*S-Y-N*, not *S-O-N*," she whispered softly. "I just moved here from Seattle, and Martika has taken me under her wing. I don't know if I'm up for the constellation work, though; it sounds too intense for me."

Finally, someone who was honest about it! I wished I'd been told what was going to happen so I could've at least had the sense to run away. I guess it ended up being a good thing, although I wasn't sure if I could ever do it again.

I didn't hear most of the other introductions because I was trying so hard to think of the perfect thing to say when it was my turn, and I kept running through all the options in my head. I was deathly afraid of public speaking, and I probably wouldn't have agreed to come to dinner if I'd known that I had to make a speech. As my turn approached, I became even more nervous, and when the person next to me stopped speaking, all eyes turned to me, and everyone patiently waited for me to begin.

"Hello, my name is Scott," I finally said after a long silence. "Hans told me I'm supposed to be dead."

Nearly everyone in the room burst into laughter, and I too caught myself smiling, while quickly checking to make sure Hans wasn't in the room. I wasn't upset because I could feel that they were all using their laughter and warmth to cradle and support me, as they genuinely seemed to care.

I hadn't been sure if people would understand what I meant, but as I looked at the smiling faces, I recognized many from the constellation, and they seemed to remember what had happened. "And thank you, Martika," I continued, "for being so supportive since I've moved to Ashland, and for including me tonight with your family and friends."

The dinner was delicious, and it was the first time I'd been able to eat a full meal since the soul retrieval. I had been eating mostly bread and raw vegetables after the disappointing turkey-and-Swiss incident, and this meal of fresh angel-hair pasta with tomatoes and basil was an absolute feast. The food embodied love and happiness, and my soul felt nourished and rejuvenated. It was one of the most satisfying meals I'd ever had, and I could feel Martika's love and support with every bite. When the dessert of fresh blueberries arrived, everyone switched places and I was fortunate enough to end up across from Madisyn with a *y*. With the benefit of proximity, I could see that she had light blue eyes and a small white flower in her hair that complemented Martika's.

"This food feels amazing," Madisyn said as she sat down.

"Did you say *feels?*" I asked.

"Yes, the energy here is so beautiful, and this food is filled with good intention."

"I agree. I didn't know anyone else could feel energy in food. I just discovered it myself recently—

I tried to eat in a restaurant and couldn't, because it felt like I was eating someone else's anger."

She nodded. "I don't understand why more restaurants aren't into conscious cooking. That's the main reason I can't eat out anymore."

"'Conscious cooking'? I didn't know it had a name. Is that a new thing?"

"It's been around since the beginning of time. It's just that most restaurants don't care about intention. That's why a home-cooked meal always tastes better." She caught her breath for a moment and then added, "If I had a restaurant, I'd force the employees to go home if they came to work in a bad mood. You can't have a restaurant and let chefs put their bad energy in the food that's served to customers. I guess now I have to start my own restaurant! Do I have to do *everything* myself?" She laughed and her blue eyes sparkled.

I had never met someone who effortlessly balanced strength with compassion as much as she did. In her world, it appeared that both were part of a single continuum; and I was genuinely impressed with the grace with which she wove them together.

"That's a handsome bracelet." She changed the subject without missing a beat while nodding to the bracelet Robert had given me.

"Thanks. A friend of mine made it for me."

"Tell me about it."

"It's made of carnelian and has moonstone and silver because of my connection to the moon. It comforts me."

"Oh, that makes sense," she smiled. "I thought I felt some lunar energy coming from you. I have a spiritual jewelry company. This is a piece of mine." She gestured toward the necklace she was wearing. It had three silver ovals with Chinese characters and a clear crystal hanging from it.

"It's very beautiful."

"Yes, I love it. I just licensed it from a friend of Martika's. I've actually been looking for some new designs that can be worn by men. Maybe your friend would be interested in working with me."

"That would be great—I'll let him know." I thought that getting Robert some additional income would allow him to spend less time at the Co-op begging for money, and have more quality guru time.

"Give me your number and I'll call you when we're ready to take on some more designs. In the meantime, find out if your friend might be interested."

"I will." I gave her my number, hoping that she wouldn't wait too long to call. As I handed her the paper, a friend of hers appeared and whispered in her ear.

"That's my ride," Madisyn said while getting up. "I have to go now. It was really nice talking to you."

"You, too."

"Bye, Lunar Boy." She winked as she walked toward the door.

"Goodbye." I nearly blushed.

After Madisyn left, I realized that I still hadn't fully recovered from Yreka and was starting to get tired. I decided it was probably a good time to leave and found Martika outside on her porch saying goodbye to the other guests. I too said my goodbyes and walked down her painted white steps into the night and toward my apartment.

There were no streetlamps on the road until I got to the main arterial, but the moon was full, which provided plenty of light. Walking alone by the light of the moon was a perfect way to end such a wonderful evening. When I arrived at my apartment, I immediately crawled into bed, filled with gratitude to finally be part of a community that welcomed me so completely. I closed my eyes and fell asleep, the happiest I'd been in years.

CHAPTER ELEVEN

After I returned from Yreka, my sleep patterns never completely went back to normal. I'd been having nightmares about Cheryl's accident for years, but the traumatic experience in Yreka took my nightmares to an entirely new level. Tapping into a fear from my infancy that I'd blocked out before I could even walk, the dreams shook me to my very core. And as the weeks progressed, I began dreading falling asleep because the inevitable flashbacks to that day in Yreka were sure to return. Robert attempted to assure me that I was safe, but I still felt that whatever was after me seemed to get closer when I was sleeping.

scoʇʇ blum

After nearly two full weeks of violently disturbed sleep, I began to get really worried and started to obsessively research what dreams meant and how they could be controlled. The lack of rest was definitely affecting my waking hours, and I was increasingly becoming unsure of the line that separated the two. I resorted to browsing nearly every bookshelf in the library and was finally relieved to discover a book about lucid dreaming, which outlined in very practical terms the tools needed to control dreams. I hoped that if I could remain in control, I would be able to put mine in their place and finally get an uninterrupted night's rest.

I started by explicitly following the instructions in the book, and before I went to sleep, I would set the intention to meet my dream guides as soon as I was unconscious. I chose to hold on to the idea of my ancestors from the constellation because they were the only people I knew who were dead besides Cheryl. I was hoping that they would accept my invitation, since I'd only briefly met them at the constellation and had never spent much time with them while they were still alive.

I wasn't very successful at first, and every time I tried to influence my dreams, I would either wake up or get sucked into another flashback of Yreka. What finally worked was to imagine standing in one place and spinning around really fast as soon as I began dreaming. Once I stopped spinning, I would still be dreaming and would remain in control. After a few nights of practice, I was able to direct my dreams without spinning.

When I finally arrived in my first lucid dream state, I nearly tripped over an older man seated in a weathered wooden rocking chair. We were on the porch of a familiar gray house with a white picket fence bordering a huge cornfield that I thought I recognized but couldn't place. It was nearly dusk, and the air was warm and humid, with the buzzing sound of crickets filling the silence. After a few moments of taking in the scene, I recognized the porch as a house in Iowa my grandmother had taken me to when I'd visited her as a child. The house had been about to be torn down, and she had wanted to show me where she'd grown up.

"Hello, Scott," the older gentleman on the porch said as he kept the rocking chair in motion with his large bare feet.

I stared at him blankly.

"I'm your great-grandfather."

"Oh, sorry. I didn't recognize you."

"That's okay—you never saw me when we were on the same plane before."

He had died in a hunting accident before I was born, which probably explained why my grandmother had been so upset when she'd found out that my father wanted to give me a gun for my thirteenth birthday. Nobody had really talked about my great-grandfather when I was growing up, and the only time I'd ever met him was at the constellation when he was represented by a woman.

"You've been spending a lot of time here," my great-grandfather continued. "Don't you like living on Earth?"

"It's okay, I guess." I had never thought about it before. "I suppose I was just drawn here to discover something."

"What are you looking for?"

"I don't know. But it seems important."

"Yes, it is. You are starting to pay attention to your intuition, which is good. You will come to find it is the only sense you can rely on. Your eyes and ears are easily deceived, but your intuition is your compass."

At that moment, the white picket fence that surrounded the house morphed into a brightly colored cement wall that was painted in alternating rectangles of primary colors. The lawn turned to sand before my very eyes, and a silver metal slide and seesaw grew out of it within seconds. I instantly recognized the playground as the one from the pre-school I had attended during my early childhood years. When I looked back to my great-grandfather, I saw that his house had been replaced by a low-slung gray stucco schoolhouse.

"Where are we?" I yelled over the echoes of childhood screams that began to fill the playground.

"We are in your dreamland."

"My dreamland? What's here?"

"Whatever you want to be. You can use it to work on earthly problems and find the best solutions before returning. It's also a good way to stay in touch with the spirit plane while you're on Earth."

Although none of this seemed to make sense logically, I could feel in my heart that what he was saying was true. "So this is the spirit plane?"

"No, this is a safe zone between consciousness and the spirit plane. Many of the same rules apply, but nobody can get in unless you invite them here."

"Can I get to the spirit plane from here?"

"Yes, you can, but you aren't ready yet. I suggest you spend some time here and get familiar with your dreamland first. If you're still interested, we can talk about that later."

Spending time in my dreamland was a lot of fun. I could conjure almost any time and place I wanted and meet friends and relatives from the past at whatever age I wanted them to be. I started with my favorite memories, reliving them one at a time: The first time I learned to ride a bicycle. My first puppy. The vacation to Yosemite. One after another, I revisited these moments until I couldn't remember any more.

Then I began to conjure my worst memories and change them into good ones. I visited my first day of first grade, where I wet my pants during recess. I found I could *will* a different course of events if I tried hard enough. So I made sure to use the bathroom before I went to class, and by the time recess came around, I was completely dry and played on the seesaw without incident. I ran through my bad memories and fixed them all. I could reinvent my past, and although I knew it hadn't actually changed the course of my own history, I became much more at ease with myself. It was comforting to know that I could learn from my mistakes.

But there was one thing I couldn't figure out.

"Why can't I relive memories with Cheryl?" I asked my great-grandfather.

"As I mentioned before, you are able to invite people and places into your dreamland at will. But those people and places have to accept your invitation before coming in. The souls of people you conjure actually participate in your dreams."

"But why wouldn't she want to come in? Even people I haven't seen since preschool come."

"You trapped Cheryl in your dreamland for many years, and she was unable to progress to where she needed to be. At the moment, she's a bit wary of returning here."

"How could I trap her here when she needed to accept my invitation to come?"

"Well, of course she accepted it at first—you had a very special bond. But once she arrived, you kept her here by sinking your energetic hooks in her."

"Really? Why would I do that?"

"There are many reasons to attach to other people's energy. In your case, it was out of fear that you were going to lose a part of yourself when she died."

His words struck a chord in me that I knew was true. The more I understood, the more I felt awful about what I had done to Cheryl after she died.

"Don't be so hard on yourself," my great-grandfather said. "It's actually a pretty common situation for many people who love each other."

"Is she mad at me?"

"I doubt it. You just need to give her some space until she gets her own afterlife established, and I'm sure she'll visit you in the future once she's more settled."

I realized that one of the main things keeping my interest in the dreamland alive was the search for Cheryl. Once I discovered that she wasn't to be found, I began to get bored. I asked my great-grandfather about showing me the spirit plane again, and although he told me I still wasn't ready, he could tell I was getting close. Eventually he agreed to help me prepare.

"The first thing you have to do is learn to protect yourself energetically from other souls," he began. "Here you don't have the barrier of a body to shield yourself from energy outside your soul, so you need to learn to contain yourself."

"Contain myself? What does that mean?"

"You need to surround yourself with protective white light so that it only lets good energy in. You'll still be able to feel everything, but there won't be any serious damage, like what happened in Yreka."

"You know about that?"

"Of course. I was with you that day. I've been walking with you since you were born. You just didn't pay attention."

I wondered why it had taken me so long to let my ancestors help me. I'd always felt that it was more noble to be on my own, but I began to understand that drawing from the strength of family felt quite natural.

"Do you believe in evil?" I was still trying to come to terms with what seemed like a simple idea, but it became more complicated the more I thought about it. "I'm not sure if I believe we are all good *and* evil, or if evil is outside of me. I guess if we were all one, then I wouldn't need protection, right?"

"Not necessarily. The truth lies somewhere in between. Yes, it's true we are all one, but it's also about relative power. Relative strength."

"What do you mean?"

"For example, if a negative force is drawing from all the negative energy of humanity and you are drawing only from your own positive energy, it's likely you would be overpowered."

"Like I was in Yreka?"

"Exactly. Eventually, you will learn to harness *like energy* from other souls that are in solidarity with you. But I don't recommend you try to do that now, since you'll have to leave yourself open and vulnerable in order to align yourself with others. You need more experience to be able to discern who is helpful and who is not."

"So what should I do?"

"For now, you should simply protect yourself. As you grow in your own personal power, you will naturally attract others with like interests, but after what happened to you in Yreka, you should probably be extra careful as you have already attracted some attention you don't want."

"Will you show me how to protect myself?" I definitely didn't want to go through another Yreka experience.

"It's quite simple. Just imagine yourself surrounded by a bubble of white light and relax. The more you do so, the more the white light will fill your soul and protect you."

"But where does the white light come from?"

"It comes from within. White is made up of *all* the colors, which are all inside you. By releasing the energy of them simultaneously, you both cleanse and protect yourself from unwanted energy as they blend together into the color white."

It all seemed very abstract and complicated, and I became frustrated as I tried to remember mixing paint in summer-school art class. "I don't think I'm doing it right."

"That's because you're thinking too much. Simply *feel* protected. *Feel* safe. Don't let your mind get in the way. The colors will take care of themselves. Just relax and feel secure. I'm right here. I won't let you down."

As I quieted my breathing and imagined feeling safe and protected, I began to sense a warm glow emanating deep from within. It filled me slowly at first, and when I opened my eyes, it looked like I was standing under a very bright lightbulb. But I could see that the light was literally coming from within me. Its energy illuminated nearly two feet in all directions, and it felt very comforting. The more I relaxed, the brighter the light got, but when I started to think about what was happening, it would dim. And although it was unusual to see myself lit up like a lightbulb, it also felt very natural.

"Good," my great-grandfather said. "Practice that regularly, and once you get used to your light, I'll take you to the other side. Protection is very important on the spirit plane—we don't want anything bad to happen."

I spent the next few days practicing surrounding myself with protective light, and as I did so, I became less afraid of going to sleep at night. It finally felt that I had the tools to keep myself safe and protected if something horrible happened again like it had in Yreka.

I also changed my diet significantly. I had to stop eating at restaurants completely because I could no longer trust that the employees would be in a good mood when they prepared my food. And since I would ingest their energy when I ate, their mood became mine. I had never learned to cook for myself, but I had no choice now because of how sensitive I'd become.

In addition to my emotional sensitivity, my body also seemed to be changing—I could no longer digest rich foods very easily. I radically simplified my diet to the point of eating only steamed brown rice and drinking red rooibos tea. It was very cleansing, and although I didn't have a lot of energy when I started, after a while I felt better than I ever had. I knew it wasn't very healthy in the long run, but those were the only things I could keep in my stomach with all the shifts that were happening. I also felt that the more weight I began to lose, the easier it was to stay in my dreamland.

The extra pounds seemed to weigh me down, and the leaner I became, the more freedom I had to slip in and out of consciousness.

When the day to begin exploring the spirit world finally arrived, my great-grandfather took me to a part of my dreamland that I'd never seen before. We walked past the playground of my pre-school, across the freeway overpass of my adolescence, and over the mountain pass of my teenage years. On the other side of the mountain range, we approached the edge of a massive cliff that was so high above the valley floor that I couldn't see the bottom. All that was visible was a field of clouds that went on for miles, with birds flying in and out of the billowy mist like dolphins playing in the surf. I thought I had explored my dreamland thoroughly before, but I didn't remember this particular precipice. It was as if it had appeared out of nowhere when I was ready to see it, and it seemed to beckon me with clouds that were breaking like waves against the cliff. As I stood mesmerized by the awesome beauty in front of me, a small flock of large ravens circled above my head and cast an ominous shadow at my feet.

"Ravens signal change," my great-grandfather said.

"They always seem to follow me," I laughed.

"That's because they are also your spirit animal. You have much change to experience in this lifetime, and the ravens will help keep you on track. They act like signposts to indicate you're on the right path."

He took my left hand with his right, and raised his other straight out. Intuitively I mirrored his gesture as we walked to the edge of the cliff.

"Are you ready?" he asked.

I nodded, and we both jumped off the cliff together. As soon as our feet left the ground, we plummeted toward the valley below, and my stomach caught in my throat. I felt a twinge of panic as we quickly passed through the clouds and I could see the valley floor rapidly approaching. My great-grandfather gently squeezed my hand, and his expression told me that everything was going to be okay. I focused on his warm smile and deep, knowing eyes and felt my shoulders begin to relax.

As calmness filled the rest of my body, our free fall gracefully flowed into an arc-like flight that began to curve upward toward the clouds above. When we broke through the cloud cover, the misty whiteness was replaced by a rainbow of crystal-like light beams that shifted and undulated through an ocean of amoebalike pockets of energy. And when I looked over to my great-grandfather, I was surprised to find that he had also transformed into a formless energy membrane. But it was strange because I could almost recognize him more easily without his body than I could *with* it. It was as if I were finally seeing the real him, without the arbitrary noise of the physical world cluttering his soul.

We continued to fly through the vivid colors with an ease and freedom that was absolutely exhilarating. However, it wasn't actually like flying; it was more like swimming—swimming in a sea of souls. And since mine was also free of my body, I was able to feel things with much more intensity than I could on Earth. It was as if I had been wearing dirty sunglasses all my life and was finally able to look at a sunset for the first time without protection.

But it wasn't just seeing and feeling. All of my senses became one, and I could simultaneously see/hear/feel/smell/taste everything surrounding me. My Earth senses were tiny little holes that only let in a portion of what was around me, and I was nearly overwhelmed by my ability to sense with my entire being. There was no difference between seeing and feeling and tasting and hearing and smelling. There was only *being* and *sensing*.

"This is incredible!" I said to my great-grand-father telepathically, which felt more natural than my vocal cords ever had. Speaking was as simple as thinking, and I no longer had to worry about vocabulary obscuring my thoughts.

"Yes, it is. This is pure energy. The essence of life without the limitations of the physical world. The physical world has many advantages, but nothing compares to the immediacy of the spiritual plane. Philosophers have long written about the importance of living in the moment, but here you don't really have a choice."

"That's for sure." It was easy to understand what he meant. Everything was in constant motion, and I was compelled to be aware of every moment that was happening to me. However, the thing that took the most time to get used to was the lack of personal space. The edges of my soul overlapped with those of others', which felt a bit claustrophobic at first. But soon I was comforted by the feeling of floating in the sea of souls, which was like a familiar fabric that had been stitched together into a massive, undulating quilt.

At first I was cautious and stayed near my great-grandfather. But as I became more confident, I would wander farther and farther away from him before returning to his side. The more I got used to being in the spirit world, the more fun I had with simply moving around. Since gravity wasn't nearly as confining as it was on Earth, I felt like a kid again, sliding in my socks on my aunt's hardwood floors. Of course, since there wasn't any of the friction from my socks (or from my feet, for that matter), I could slide through the sea of souls for what seemed to be miles without slowing.

After one particularly long slide, I found myself unable to slow down and actually felt like I was accelerating far away from my great-grandfather. I called out to him . . . right before I recognized the dark entity that was rapidly approaching. In the instant I sensed what was happening, it started to pull me swiftly toward its dark core. I swirled in circles as the dark energy cords began to entwine my soul and pull me closer. Thankfully, my great-grandfather appeared and took control of the situation.

"Scott, protect yourself with your white light! You've let it fade, and you don't have any protection!"

I looked down and saw that he was right: my light was completely extinguished. I tried to conjure it from within, but my panic prevented me from focusing.

"I can't!" I screamed. "It's not working!"

"Just calm down and relax. Your strength remains inside you. Just remember what we practiced and let it come."

Remarkably, I *was* able to relax when I tuned in to the confidence my ancestors had in me. My great-grandfather taught me many skills, but his unconditional faith in me brought me more strength than I ever thought possible. Within moments, a wave of calm filled my soul, and I sensed the familiar feeling of my inner light protecting me with a white bubble. As soon as the bubble congealed, I felt it bounce me off of my trajectory and away from the darkness. My great-grandfather followed me closely, and when we finally settled down far away from the danger, he gave me one final reminder.

"You should remember to check in with your protection regularly until it becomes second nature. At first it's easy to let your guard down and forget to keep it illuminated, but after a while it will simply become a part of you. But as you can see, it's very slippery here, and mistakes that are made will last for eternity."

Even after the scare, I still became increasingly preoccupied with spending as much time in the spirit world as possible, and the return to consciousness was much less interesting than it used to be. I didn't leave my house unless I absolutely had to, and I found myself less interested in other people who were trapped in their physical bodies. I knew that Robert and Martika would probably understand what I was going through, but I didn't want to stay conscious long enough to see them. Life on Earth seemed so archaic with my minuscule sensory holes that let in a fraction of the world around me, and I found the physical manifestation of bodies to be entirely cumbersome and inelegant.

I was rapidly becoming bored with all that the earthly plane had to offer, and was genuinely annoyed when I started to receive late notices in the mail because I hadn't kept up with the financial obligations of living a "comfortable" life in the physical world. There was a part of me that wanted to remain a responsible citizen, but mostly I couldn't stop thinking about the other side whenever I was burdened with consciousness.

After returning to the spirit world, I began to take a much more deliberate approach to exploring my surroundings. I was most fascinated with the other souls I was in constant contact with, although every time I tried to communicate with them, I found it nearly impossible. Everyone's thoughts were as tangible as any other part of them, but they all mingled together, and it was difficult to discern one from another. It was like trying to listen to whispers in a crowd while standing next to a waterfall.

From the beginning, I was easily able to tune in to my great-grandfather, since I was already familiar with his energy; however, souls I didn't know were much more challenging. My great-grandfather explained that the problem was that on Earth I was used to multitasking, constantly juggling many things at once to save time. In the spirit plane, everything that ever existed was completely accessible and in constant motion, so it wasn't possible to concentrate on more than one thing at a time without becoming overwhelmed.

With his help, I retrained myself to be fully present, and once I did, I began to have some of the most profound conversations I'd ever had, even within the simplest of salutations. I could sense that everyone wanted to be heard fully and completely, and quickly realized that I had been missing out on the majority of what was going on around me by constantly "multitasking" my focus away from what was truly happening.

After a while, I became much more comfortable with the basics of spending time on the spirit plane, and the more often we returned, the more crowded it became. And after the fifth time, the souls were so dense that it was nearly impossible to move.

"This is becoming a popular place," I noticed.

"*You* are the popular one," said my great-grandfather. "Souls are coming from the far ends of the spirit world to be near you."

"What's so special about me? Is it because I'm new here?"

"That's part of it, but the main reason is because you are surrounded in white light. Your energy makes them feel good, and they want to be near it."

"But they can surround themselves with their own white light. Don't they know that it's inside them already?"

"Unfortunately, they don't. Most people think happiness comes from outside themselves, and here it's no different. It's one of the great tragedies of life, and the reason why so many live without joy for most of their days."

"But it's so easy. You should teach them how to do it, like you did me."

"That is not my destiny. I am happy to help you with whatever you need, but I'm not interested in helping *everyone*. Perhaps that is your path."

At that instant, a small soul floated near, and as it brushed up against me, I could sense its life history. The more time I spent in the spirit world, the longer I was able to focus my attention on a particular soul and *read* its energy. It was like an internal knowing, and the more open the soul was, the more I could intuit. It seemed strange that I could sense if one was small or large, old or young, happy or sad, but I could. There was a sense of knowing that was more certain than anything I'd *thought* I'd known on Earth.

The small soul belonged to a young boy who'd lost his parents in a house fire. After bouncing from one unloving foster home to another, he'd died at the tender age of seven after he caught pneumonia in the dead of winter. He was lost and scared and didn't understand why he was there.

"What's your name?" I asked.

"Tamlin."

"Tamlin, you don't need to be scared. Do you want to surround yourself with white light like me?"

"Uh-huh."

"The secret is that it's already inside you. Think good thoughts, and remember the love of your parents. They still care about you and want you to be happy." I didn't know where my words were coming from, but as I let them flow, they seemed to comfort him.

Slowly, a small glowing white light began to flicker inside of Tamlin's soul. It was smaller than a grain of sand at first, but gradually got bigger. Instinctively, I reached in and gently coaxed the light until it became bright enough to surround him. His soul began to feel lighter and happier until much of his sadness had faded. Within seconds, his parents appeared from the crowd and embraced him.

"Where have you been?" asked the young boy, his soul emanating both anger and elation.

"We've been looking for you everywhere," said his mother. "You were always a beacon of light on Earth, but here we couldn't find you although we knew you were here somewhere. As soon as we saw your light a few moments ago, we knew we'd finally found you."

"I don't think I'm needed here anymore." My great-grandfather smiled as he began to fade away. "Call out if you need me."

I spent more and more time in the spirit world and helped as many souls as I could. It seemed very natural to me, and I felt that I was doing what I was born to do. I was bringing many souls joy and happiness, and I could tell that I was genuinely making a difference. It was an immensely powerful experience, and every time I returned, there would be more and more damaged souls waiting to be healed. I had finally found my soul's purpose, and it was extremely rewarding to be able to do something so meaningful.

Occasionally I would catch a glimpse of Cheryl, but she kept her distance and simply waved. It was nice seeing her again, but I wasn't obsessed like I'd been previously. I was content to let her be, and knew that she would approach me when she was ready. And as I spent more time in my unconscious world, I began to recognize a little girl who was often near the edge of the cliff to the spirit world. She had a familiar energy, but I couldn't remember where she might be from.

After a while, I began to look forward to seeing her, and we both traded smiles whenever we saw each other. At first I wasn't sure if she was dark or light because of how powerful her energy was, but as the days progressed, I could sense that she was friendly. Finally, I worked up the courage to ask her who she was.

"Hi," I finally greeted her.

"Hello," she said matter-of-factly.

"Who are you?"

"My name is Autumn. I am your daughter."

With that, she giggled playfully and right before my eyes turned into a bright blue dragonfly and hovered a few inches from my nose.

"You're my daughter?!" I exclaimed while staring dumbfounded into the eyes of the dragonfly.

And over the fluttering of her translucent wings, I heard her giggle once more as she darted away in a blur.

CHAPTER TWELVE

After I first spoke with Autumn, my mind filled with dozens of questions, like: *When is she going to be born? How long has she been waiting for me?* and more important, *If I am her father, who is her mother?*

I saw her a few more times in my dreamland, but more and more I would sense her presence when I briefly returned to consciousness for food, water, and bathroom breaks. It was as if she was preparing to be born and wanted to begin exploring what the physical plane was all about.

One evening when I uncharacteristically spent the entire night on Earth, I sat outside on my back porch and watched the moon rise and cast some of the most beautiful shadows I had ever seen onto the trees of my backyard. After it had fully revealed itself, I could sense the familiar feeling of Autumn nearby. When I looked around, I saw that the moonlight and shadows had coalesced into the shape of a giant bunny within the twisted branches of the large plum tree.

"Autumn?" I asked aloud. "Is that you?"

The ears of the rabbit began moving as if they were waving to me, and just when I was about to write it off as my imagination playing tricks on me, I noticed that the air was as still as could be. There wasn't even a light breeze in the warm summer air, and all the surrounding branches were completely motionless as the bunny ears continued to wave.

My stomach filled with the giddiness of a thousand butterflies, and I watched the dancing bunny in the branches of the plum tree for nearly half an hour. When my attention began to wane, Autumn sensed my distraction and instantly morphed into a graceful swan that appeared to float on the reflection of the silver moonlight. She then choreographed an intricate production of various animals dancing in the tree one after another for the next several hours. Swans transformed into giraffes. Giraffes turned into polar bears. Polar bears into chickens. Chickens into cats. I was impressed by her creativity and ingenuity, but it was her playfulness and genuine innocence that captured my heart.

By then, the more time I spent in the spirit world, the less food I seemed to need. But even with my limited meals, I had finally run out of brown rice and red tea. For the first time since I'd begun spending time in the spirit world, I needed to reenter the physical one to replenish my supplies. Although I was definitely nervous about coming into contact with other people again, I was excited to share my news with Robert and was hoping to get his perspective on Autumn. After I prepared mentally, I instinctively put on a long-sleeved shirt, a hat, and sunglasses to protect myself from the outside world and ventured back to the Co-op. This time I knew for sure that Robert would be there and wondered if his sign would give me any answers.

Without saying hello, I walked right up to him and read his new sign aloud.

There are no straight lines in nature.

"Be honest," I joked. "You make those signs for me, don't you?"

"Of course not." Out the corner of my eye, I thought I saw Robert wink at Puppy Don. "You'll know when a sign is meant for you."

"How do you come up with all those sayings?"

"They are given to me by those who need to be heard. And I record them for those who need to hear. And sometimes they're the same person."

"I see." I wondered silently if he ever wrote anything *I* had said. Then I recounted my recent adventures in the hopes that he had some insight.

"So you finally met Autumn?" Robert asked after I finished. "What did you think about her?"

"She's quite playful!"

"Yes, she is that." He laughed.

"You know her?"

"I met her during your soul retrieval."

"Why didn't you tell me?"

"I don't think you could have handled me telling you about your unborn daughter then. You already had a pretty full day."

"Yeah, I guess so."

"It looks like you've spent a lot of time on the other side, haven't you?"

"True. How did you know that?"

"Because you're entirely out of your body right now. At least two feet above and one foot to the left. You need to try to stay grounded while you're on Earth or you won't have a choice."

"A choice of what?"

"Of where you live. Do you want to live on this planet or the spirit plane?"

"Why do I have to choose? Can't I just continue to visit?"

"I think you've been more than visiting, haven't you?"

"I just feel so powerful when I'm there. And I'm definitely helping many souls heal. My life seems so much more meaningful in the spirit world. It's as if I was made to heal others."

"Yes, you do have a gift. But it will always be with you. Living on this planet is also a gift, and you have a lot to do here as well. It's your choice, and you're lucky enough to have another chance to decide."

"You mean it's not the first time I've had to choose?"

"Everyone is faced with the same choice imme-diately after they're born. Souls enter their human bodies in the womb, and most of the time they stay there until birth. And when they're born, they have to decide if they're ready to deal with the limita-tions of living here. The few who don't want to be here decide to leave, and that's what is commonly referred to as SIDS."

"Sudden infant death syndrome?"

"Yes. It's an ironic name since it's nowhere near sudden. The transition itself is instantaneous, but the decision takes many weeks to make. That's the main thing we all go through as soon as we're born into this world: deciding if we're ready to be limited by these bodies in order to experience life here."

"But why would anyone want to live here? There are so many things wrong with this place. And these bodies *are* so limited compared to the spiritual plane."

"Because there are many experiences and les-sons that can only be had here."

"Like what?"

"Like having children, for one."

My thoughts returned to Autumn, and I began to wonder what it would be like to be a father. There was something deep inside me that wanted to care for her and teach her about life on this planet. Almost more than anything I'd ever wanted to do.

"Why can't I live in both places like I have been?"

"Because your body can't handle it. The more time you spend there, the more you'll disregard your body, and it will eventually die. How long do you think it's been since you left your apartment?"

"I don't know . . . maybe a week."

"More like *three*. Look at yourself. You must have lost fifteen to twenty pounds. Your spirit is hovering above your body like a helium balloon, and your pants are nearly falling to your ankles."

"Yeah, I should probably eat more, but I don't think it's been three weeks."

"Look at this," he said as he showed me a newspaper.

The date said September 10. I was shocked. It had been nearly five weeks since I'd gone to Martika's party. That explained the stacks of late notices and threats from utility companies that my mailbox could barely contain.

"You have to choose," he repeated, and this time his words went right to my core.

"But what about Autumn? What would she do if I don't stay?"

"She'll be fine. Autumn is a powerful soul, and she'll be okay with whatever choice you make. She has many options, so you don't have to worry about her. This isn't her first time here, and she knows what she's doing. But you'll miss out on one of the most incredible joys of the universe if you decide to leave now. Your work on the other side will remain forever, but the joy of children is a very special opportunity that doesn't happen every day."

"When will I meet her mother?"

"After your soul decides to stay. Now, go into the store and get yourself some food. You look like you're about to pass out."

I stocked up on extra brown rice and rooibos, and after waving goodbye to Robert and Puppy Don, I made the familiar journey back up the hill. When I was nearly halfway home, I noticed three dragonflies that seemed to be following me. There was something very familiar about them, especially the two that were closest to me. By then I was used to Autumn's games, and naturally assumed she was one of them.

"So Autumn, who are your two friends?" I was used to speaking to her out loud, no matter what form she took. I stopped in the middle of the street, and the three dragonflies began circling above me. The path they followed moved closer and closer to the top of my head until it felt as if I was wearing a dragonfly crown and I was their dragonfly king. And in my heart, there was a knowing. An unspoken answer to my question that was louder than any words that could be spoken: *Daddy and Mommy.*

CHAPTER THIRTEEN

I spent the next week and a half meditating on the most important decision I'd ever have to make in this lifetime. I'd finally discovered my soul's purpose, and found I was really good at it. But I had to decide between following my calling in the spirit world and raising my unborn daughter.

The more I meditated, the more I felt that *either* decision was probably the right one. I knew my work would still be waiting for me after I was done with this planet, and I also knew in my heart that Autumn would understand if I continued on my journey before having the opportunity to see her in this dimension. And although I was honored that she had chosen me, I had to do what was right for myself because I didn't want to resent her if I decided to have a family out of obligation.

I wanted to ask Autumn what *she* thought I should do, but she had completely stopped visiting my dreams. I could definitely feel her presence in the physical world; however, I sensed she wanted me to reach my own conclusion.

I also tried to spend more time on Earth and take care of my body so I could make a balanced choice. It wasn't easy eating regularly again, but most difficult was neglecting the souls that were waiting for me. I could sense them calling and knew that I could help, but I also knew that I had to decide quickly about bringing Autumn into this world.

At dusk on the day of the next full moon, my contemplation was interrupted by a knock on my front door. When I opened it, I saw a thin, monk-like bald man wearing a white robe and a braided red necklace around his neck. At his feet was a black puppy that looked a lot like Robert's companion.

"Puppy Don?" I asked.

Then I heard Robert's distinctive voice, although it was much quieter and weaker than normal: "Yes, Scott, it's us. Can we come in?"

My eyes followed the figure's flowing white robe back up to his face, and I almost fell backward when I came to his eyes.

"Robert, is that you?"

"Of course it's me—who do you think it is?"

"Your hair . . ." I stepped aside and gestured for them to come in.

"Yes, I got a haircut."

"And a shave," I said, underlining the obvious. "You sure look different without hair."

When we were inside, we sat down at the table in the small dining room that separated the kitchen from the living room. After turning on the light above the table, I looked down at Puppy Don and noticed that he was wearing a braided red collar that matched Robert's necklace. I instinctively bent down to take a closer look and recoiled when I recognized the braids from Robert's recently departed locks.

"You made a necklace from your hair?!" My face scrunched up—I couldn't hide my disgust.

Robert simply nodded as he proceeded to attach a thin white thread connecting his necklace to Puppy Don's collar. Characteristically, the dog curled up at my friend's feet and closed his eyes. In the light I could see Robert's face much

more clearly and noted that he had circles under his sunken eyes and the corners of his mouth
curved downward.

"Are you all right?" I asked. "You don't look so
good."

He replied in a soft, scratchy voice, "It looks
like the disease in this body was further along
than I thought"—he paused long enough to sigh a
deep, heavy sigh—"and I won't be able to use it for
much longer."

"What do you mean by that? You told me that
disease was something that can be controlled at
will! You told me that anyone could do it if they
had the desire! What are you saying? You can't
leave now!" I was confused and angry. Robert was
the only person who knew everything I was going
through, and I wasn't ready to be without him.

"You don't even know if you're going to stay
on this planet. And if you do, you're going to have
Autumn."

"But why can't you just heal your body? You
said you could do that."

"I thought I could, but this one is too far gone.
And besides, my work in Ashland is done. You
don't need me anymore."

"Of course I need you! You can't leave yet." I knew it was pointless to beg, but I felt desperate.

"I need to ask a huge favor of you," Robert said.

"Anything," I replied, wiping the tears from the sides of my cheeks.

"I need you to take care of Don. I made a promise to him that he would be taken care of while he was in this form."

"But, I don't know—"

"And if you decide to move on," he interrupted, "Martika has already agreed to take care of him. She can't this week because she's gone to San Francisco for a seminar. Could you wait on your decision until she gets back?"

"Of course." It was the least I could do after all he'd done for me.

"Thank you very much. This means a lot to both of us." He began rummaging through his cloth bag as he continued. "I don't mean to impose any more than I already have." I wanted to assure him that it was no imposition, but he waved his hand to silence me. "But out of respect for Don, I need to perform a ceremony to honor the body he has lent me and celebrate the life we have both lived in it."

I was awestruck as his words sunk in and I understood the weight of the situation. And when I looked deep into his eyes, I found something in them that I had never seen before: Gratitude. *Immense gratitude.* He glanced down at the sleeping puppy, and I could feel a graciousness—an indebtedness—that was more powerful than any words that could be spoken. And in a whisper that was nearly inaudible, he mouthed, "Thank you."

I was speechless and almost forgot that I was actually there. Although I felt completely disconnected from my body, I heard my outside voice say, "Of course. Whatever you need."

Robert smiled gently as he carefully pulled a beautiful sheet of handmade rice paper from his bag and with both hands deliberately placed it in front of him on the dining table. The veined cream-colored paper was bordered with raspberry-red flowers and a dancing yellow light that shimmered on the gold-leafed stems. He brought out a long white feather that had been carved into a pointed tip on one end, and a small jar of old-fashioned black ink.

With a long wooden match, he ceremoniously lit each of the three green tapers on my dining table. He then slowly pushed one in front of me and one in front of him and lovingly placed the third on the floor next to Puppy Don. After the candles were lit, he gestured for me to dim the lights, and once I'd done so, he closed his eyes and sat without speaking for several minutes. The only thing to break the profound silence was the gurgling sound coming from his lungs as he struggled with short, shallow breaths.

When he opened his eyes, he picked up the quill and dipped it into the jar. After letting the excess ink drip back inside, he began to inscribe the paper with long, precise strokes. From my vantage point, I couldn't read what he was writing, but I could see that his eyes were more focused than I'd ever seen them. He continued to write intensely, with a deliberate sense of purpose, pausing briefly to fill his quill with ink before writing more. When he finished, he gently placed the feather back on the table, and instinctively Puppy Don sat up and stared at him, both of his ears at attention.

Robert rose from the chair and with both hands picked up the inscribed paper and began to speak, his voice clear and powerful for the first time that night. "With this *Jisei*, our *Death Poem*, I humbly honor the life of Donald Newport and the journey we have both traveled within this worthy body.

Although flesh is merely clothing, it has served us both well and has protected and carried us on many important journeys during this lifetime."

Robert then kneeled in front of Puppy Don so they could look directly in each other's eyes and continued: "I am forever indebted to you for your generous gift, and I will now be your servant for the next three lifetimes. I will remain at your side and will give my life to yours for you to do with whatever you please."

With that, Robert placed the paper in front of Puppy Don and lowered his forehead to the floor at the base of the puppy's paws. Puppy Don then looked down at the sheet Robert had inscribed and appeared to read it. After a few minutes, he licked the side of Robert's face and let out a quiet whimper.

Robert slowly sat back up, picked up the paper, and placed it in front of me before returning to his chair.

When I looked down, I was overwhelmed by how beautiful the calligraphy was. Each stroke of his pen had lovingly caressed the paper and left a precise trail of ink that had more in common with Japanese artwork than the English language. After basking in the beauty of the script itself, I began to slowly read the haiku one word at a time, letting each of his final words sink in:

Winter's snowy shawl
That covered the trees in white
Is water again

After reading the words a second time, my eyes began to well up and a single teardrop escaped and slid off the bridge of my nose onto the last line of the poem, drowning the letters in an inky pool of black liquid. I looked up at Robert, and tears continued to stream down the sides of my face.

Robert picked up the paper and in a single motion brought one corner to the candle's flame until it caught fire. Puppy Don and I stared mesmerized at the burning poem, and I waited for Robert to flinch as the flames began to singe the hair on the back of his hand. At the very moment it was about to become uncomfortable to watch, he placed the burning poem into the pale green ceramic dish he'd retrieved from his bag. The flames slowly crawled to the edges of the paper, and within seconds the fire was extinguished, leaving a frail black scroll of charred remains in its wake.

Once again Robert rummaged through his canvas bag and pulled out another ceremonial tool. This time it was a small silver set of thread scissors. He used them to cut the thread where he had tied it to Puppy Don's collar and again where it was attached to his own red necklace. He gathered the thread in his left hand, and after returning the scissors to his bag, he walked around the table and stood immediately in front of me. I instinctively stood up and pushed the chair under the table so there was nothing between us.

"Scott, you are now the thread that ties Donald and me together," said Robert, regaining his booming voice of authority. "Whether you stay on this earthly plane or continue on your journey, you are now the connection that keeps us linked. And during the next lifetime, Donald and I would be honored if you would continue to bear this responsibility and be our guide. Your gift of sight will become even more powerful over the coming seasons, and you will be able to recognize both of us in an instant, no matter what form we take. Scott, will you accept this responsibility?"

Although I wasn't sure what I was going to be doing next week, let alone in the next lifetime,

I did feel indebted to Robert and wanted to give back to him in any way I could. I had no idea what that was going to entail, but I felt that if Robert had confidence in me, it was probably something I could do. "I would be honored," I finally said, and after I did, he clasped my hands in his and gently transferred the thread into my palm.

As I clenched my fingers around the thin white strands, they became warmer and warmer until I could feel them throbbing with both Robert and Puppy Don's energy. It felt very familiar, and I was humbled to be holding such a sacred relic of their bond. I'd known that the love between others was real, but this was the first time I could actually feel the energy of genuine love with my hands.

When I looked up, Robert was standing in front of his candle with his palms pressed together and his head bowed. "It's time for me to go," he said as he bent down to the candle and blew it out. When the flame was extinguished, the light dimmed in the room by more than half. There were still two candles lit, but his had burned much brighter than the others and was already sorely missed.

"Where are you going to be born next?" I began to shake uncontrollably.

"I'm not sure. Probably Cassadaga. There's a bright-eyed writer there who will be changing millions of hearts."

I didn't know where Cassadaga was, but I knew it wasn't near. "When are you leaving?"

"Tonight," he said, and his smile broke my heart. "Take care, Scott."

And with that, he shut the door behind him. I watched through the window as he walked down the street and turned the corner, and I was overcome with a wave of sadness.

My tears returned full force as soon as he was gone, and once the remaining candles had burned themselves out, I saw the full moon hovering outside my window. I had planned to commune with its lunar energy that night to help with my decision about Autumn, but I didn't have it in me anymore. My decision felt pointless in light of what had just happened. So I dramatically drew the window shade to prevent the silvery light from penetrating my room.

When I crawled into bed, the tears fell from my cheeks into the corners of my mouth and left their salty residue on my tongue. In that very moment I hated everything about the physical world with all its arbitrary limitations, and I just wanted to leave. However, I had promised Robert I would take care of Puppy Don at least until Martika returned. But if it hadn't been for that obligation, I would have definitely made the decision that moment to go into the spirit world and never return.

CHAPTER FOURTEEN

The next morning I woke up in a much better mood, and surprisingly my appetite had returned. I was absolutely famished for the first time in weeks and decided to take Puppy Don out for a walk so I could get a breakfast burrito at the outdoor kiosk near the park. After buying the food, I walked with him into the park and noticed that the weather was beginning to change. There was a faint chill in the air that hinted at the seasons to come, and I was surprised by how different the leaves looked.

I hadn't been to the park in a few weeks, and as we walked on the wood-chip trail, I was in awe of all the brilliant shades of orange and yellow that adorned the branches above. The park was bursting with color, as fall was definitely in full swing. And as soon as we approached the creek, we could see the fallen leaves floating on the shimmering water like lazy canoes.

Robert wasn't far from my thoughts that morning, and everything seemed to remind me of him. I found myself staring at the base of a large oak tree, and I watched as its yellowed leaves pulled themselves away from the branches that had held them in safety for many months and gracefully floated to the ground to be near their recently departed friends. I reflected on the humble grace with which Robert had departed the night before and felt honored to have witnessed such a profound ceremony.

As I watched the leaves fall to the ground, I instinctively caressed Puppy Don's ears and felt my fingers brush against the braided collar around his neck. My tears threatened to return as my emotions from the previous night began to bubble up again, but I quickly forced myself to feel grateful that our paths had crossed, no matter how briefly. Robert had made a huge impact on me in a short amount of time, and I knew in my heart that I would meet up with him again in the future.

I was feeling less sure than I had been the previous night about whether I wanted to stay on Earth or move on to the spirit world. I was fortunate to know about my work on the spirit plane, and I knew that I would be blessed with a family if I remained on Earth. But I wasn't sure which was more significant in the grand scheme of the universe. When I was alone with my quietest thoughts, I was confident that Autumn would be much more powerful spiritually than I could ever hope to be. Yet the question remained: *How can I make the most positive impact with my life?*

When we reached the end of the lower duck pond, I saw Robert's drawstring bag lying on top of a pile of leaves under a small maple tree. He must have abandoned it in the park before he left the previous night. I couldn't help myself from picking it up, and after a few seconds I instinctively untied the tattered string and peeked inside. There were several cardboard signs lettered in Robert's distinctive scrawl. I counted seven in total, and pulled each one out and carefully laid it on the lawn in front of me. Each sign was nearly identical to the next and had a single word floating in the center:

Yes.

"Typical!" I exclaimed aloud after inspecting both sides of each sign, hoping in vain to find another word hidden somewhere. Robert never seemed to answer any of my questions in a straightforward manner, and even after he left, he was as cryptic as ever.

I sat down on the lawn with the seven cardboard signs surrounding me, and I heard Robert's voice whisper, *"Fill your heart with 'Yes' and you will make the right decision."* I turned around, expecting to once again look deep into his water-blue eyes, but there was nobody nearby. I glanced down at Puppy Don—his ears were perked, and he was wide-awake for the first time since Robert had left the night before.

Suddenly, a low-flying raven came from behind us and sailed around the bend. As the sound of the flapping wings rushed past us, Puppy Don jumped up and chased after the bird. I hadn't seen the puppy move that quickly ever before. I ran after him, and as I turned the corner, he scampered up to a woman with long blonde hair wearing a knee-length light blue sweater. As I got closer, I recognized her as Madisyn with a *y* from Martika's dinner party.

"Hi!" I said.

"Hello, Lunar Boy. You have such a cute puppy," she said while gently caressing the side of his face. "What's his name?"

"Don."

She furrowed her brow. "He doesn't like that name anymore. He needs a much more distinguished one. How about Onyx? Do you like that, Onyx?"

Onyx jumped into her arms and started licking the side of her face while wagging his tail in agreement.

"I think he likes it," I laughed. And as I looked down at the eager puppy, I noticed that something looked different. Something was missing.

"His collar is gone." I tried to remain calm, but my panic began to show as I started searching on the ground for the red braided necklace.

"He doesn't need a collar," Madisyn said with a smile. "We all know who he is, don't we, Onyx?"

Onyx wagged his tail and let out a short, happy bark.

"Are you settling in to Ashland yet?" I asked.

"Yes, I am. I found a house just a few blocks from here, and I love it. It's filled with light, and it's great to be able to get to the park so quickly. I'm such a fan of nature, and being with the trees every day fills me with joy."

The three of us began walking on the path together, enjoying a comfortable silence, as if we'd all known each other for many lifetimes. And for some reason, it felt like we actually had. The soft sounds of nature melded effortlessly with those of our footsteps, and I felt for the first time in my life that everything was exactly as it should be, and as it always *was*. We continued to explore the lesser-known trails at the far end of the park, and as we made our way up a steep hill, we came to a large tree that had recently fallen across the path.

Madisyn gracefully found the easiest way to navigate around it, and without ceremony said, "There are no straight lines in nature."

"Where did you read that?" I asked, wondering if she had known Robert also.

"I didn't read it anywhere. It was a vision I had as a little girl, and I've always held it dear to my heart."

Out of nowhere a familiar bright blue dragon-fly flew down from the sky and landed on Madisyn's golden locks. It stopped fluttering its wings and steadied itself on tiny fairy legs with her every step.

"You have a fairy on your head," I smiled.

"Those are my peeps." She laughed as she extended her index finger and raised it to the top of her head so the dragonfly could climb aboard. It sauntered onto her finger, and she casually brought it between us so we could get a better look. The dragonfly posed for a few seconds, then quickly flew up into the trees.

As Madisyn passed a clearing, the light beamed through the trees onto her beautiful hair, and the blondest strands began to glow. For the first time in years, I saw a glimpse of love on the horizon and realized that I had finally let Cheryl go.

Abruptly, Madisyn stopped in the middle of the path, gazed up to the trees, and said, "I love Autumn."

I looked at her dumbfounded as truth bumps covered my entire body.

"I wish Autumn was here every day!" she exclaimed with her arms outstretched to the sky.

"Me, too," I smiled. "Me, too."

ABOUT THE AUTHOR

Scott **Blum** is the co-founder of the popular inspirational website DailyOM (**dailyom.com**). He is also a successful multimedia artist who has collaborated with several popular authors, musicians, and visual artists and has produced many critically acclaimed works, including a series featuring ancient meditation music from around the world. Scott lives in the mountains of Ashland, Oregon, with Madisyn Taylor—his wife, business partner, and soul mate.

Website: **www.scottblum.net**

Hay House Titles of Related Interest

YOU CAN HEAL YOUR LIFE,
the movie, starring Louise L. Hay & Friends
(available as a 1-DVD program and an expanded 2-DVD set)
Watch the trailer at: **www.LouiseHayMovie.com**

❧

DAILYOM: Inspirational Thoughts for a
Happy, Healthy, and Fulfilling Day, by Madisyn Taylor

THE DOLPHIN: Story of a Dreamer, by Sergio Bambaren

THE JOURNEY HOME: A Kryon Parable, by Lee Carroll

LINDEN'S LAST LIFE:
The Point of No Return Is Just the Beginning,
by Alan Cohen

SOLOMON'S ANGELS, by Doreen Virtue

❧

All of the above are available at your local bookstore,
or may be ordered by contacting Hay House (see last page).

❧

Don't miss **SUMMER'S PATH,** the prequel to
WAITING FOR AUTUMN, by Scott Blum.

Summer's Path is the remarkable story of Don Newport,
an engineer who comes face-to-face with his personal destiny
under extraordinary circumstances. After losing his job and

his health insurance, Don learns he has a terminal disease, with only a few months left to live. On his deathbed, he meets Robert, a brazen angel of death who promises to help him with a graceful exit. As Don prepares to say his last goodbyes to his loving wife, Robert attempts to change Don's perspective about his mortality and proposes an exceptionally unique option.

Robert leads Don through an astounding meditation of life and death and reveals various healing and spiritual concepts, including walk-ins, embodiment, and soul destiny. On this magical journey of self-realization, Don discovers that it's never too late to learn profound life lessons about ourselves and our loved ones.

Available from **www.scottblum.net**

We hope you enjoyed this Hay House book.
If you'd like to receive a free catalog featuring additional
Hay House books and products, or if you'd like information
about the Hay Foundation, please contact:

Hay House, Inc.
P.O. Box 5100
Carlsbad, CA 92018-5100

(760) 431-7695 or **(800) 654-5126**
(760) 431-6948 (fax) or **(800) 650-5115 (fax)**
www.hayhouse.com® • **www.hayfoundation.org**

Published and distributed in Australia by:
Hay House Australia Pty. Ltd., 18/36 Ralph St., Alexandria
NSW 2015 • *Phone:* 612-9669-4299 • *Fax:* 612-9669-4144
www.hayhouse.com.au

Published and distributed in the United Kingdom by:
Hay House UK, Ltd., 292B Kensal Rd., London W10 5BE
Phone: 44-20-8962-1230 • *Fax:* 44-20-8962-1239
www.hayhouse.co.uk

Published and distributed in the Republic of South Africa by:
Hay House SA (Pty), Ltd., P.O. Box 990, Witkoppen 2068
Phone/Fax: 27-11-467-8904 • orders@psdprom.co.za
www.hayhouse.co.za

Published in India by: Hay House Publishers India, Muskaan
Complex, Plot No. 3, B-2, Vasant Kunj, New Delhi 110 070
Phone: 91-11-4176-1620 • *Fax:* 91-11-4176-1630
www.hayhouse.co.in

Distributed in Canada by:
Raincoast, 9050 Shaughnessy St., Vancouver, B.C. V6P 6E5
Phone: (604) 323-7100 • *Fax:* (604) 323-2600
www.raincoast.com